Advance Praise

"A dynamic and fun read from beginning to end that touches on all of the elements of YA fiction today, while also dealing with issues of being different—being rare in one's world or another world. I thoroughly enjoyed it!"

— Laura Manfre, Co-Founder and President at Sofia Sees Hope

"*Retina Boy* is a great read! It's a fast-paced story which brings elements of science fiction and science fact to a fun and satisfying conclusion. The fact that it covers up-to-date human genetics (and bands and music) is a bonus enriching the story. The ending, complete in itself, leaves you wanting to hear what happens next. Highly recommended for young adults and above."

— Dr. Stephen Daiger, Director of the Laboratory for Molecular Diagnosis of Inherited Eye Diseases at The University of Texas Health Science Center

"This interplanetary tale, rooted in the author's real world experience with the Foundation Fighting Blindness, is a reminder to all of us that physical disabilities do not prevent us from leading extraordinary lives. Life has its high notes, and its low notes, but *Retina Boy* reminds us they're all part of a great song. *Retina Boy* is a fun read for people of all abilities."

— Dr. Shannon Boye, Associate Professor at the University of Florida

"With Retina Boy, Shaberman brings us on an adventurous journey exploring friendship, young love and quests into the unknown...a fun and delightful read."

— Dr. Laura Brady, Head of Research at Fighting Blindness Ireland

"Retina Boy is an intriguing story with characters who are compelling, resourceful and tenacious. It's an entertaining and thought-provoking novel."

— Dr. Jacque Duncan, Retinal Specialist and Professor at University of California, San Francisco Medical Center

Retina Boy

Retina Boy

Ben Shaberman

Apprentice
House Press
Loyola University Maryland

First Edition

Paperback ISBN: 978-1-62720-225-1
Ebook ISBN: 978-1-62720-226-8

Printed in the United States of America

Designed by Cara Hullings
Edited and promoted by Rayonna Burton-Jernigan
Author photo by Sarah Kioko, Kuzmak Photography Studio.

Published by Apprentice House Press

Apprentice House Press
Loyola University Maryland
4501 N. Charles Street
Baltimore, MD 21210
410.617.5265 • 410.617.2198 (fax)
www.ApprenticeHouse.com
info@ApprenticeHouse.com

For Gordon, Lulie, Ben, Beverly, and Eliot

Chapter 1

Kathy Downs struggled to rouse herself for several minutes. Something kept pulling her under, away from consciousness. Slowly, the force relented. As she awakened, she wondered if she had been in an accident or sedated for a medical procedure.

She eventually realized she was in the hospital nursery, sitting in a chair against the back wall. Kathy looked at her watch—it was almost two o'clock in the morning. She was horrified to think she had dozed off in the middle of her shift. After four months of working overnights in the newborn nursery at the Polk County Hospital in West Des Moines, Kathy had adjusted to the late hours. A large dark roast coffee with an espresso shot from Java Joe's—she was often the downtown store's last customer of the evening—was her secret weapon to getting through the night. But even when the shift was a struggle early on, before she adopted her coffee habit, Kathy had never fallen asleep on the job. And she couldn't understand why she wasn't at the nurse's station but instead in the back of the room sitting in a chair.

Thankfully, there were only three newborns on the unit that night: Doug Anderson, Joelle Pierce, and Nicole Duncan. Feeling woozy, Kathy took slow, short steps over to the bassinets to check on the babies. Though all were fast asleep, the Anderson baby was turned in the opposite direction of the others. His head faced the front wall of the nursery, which had a small window to let in some natural light. Normally, all the babies had their heads facing the back wall. Kathy shook her head in bewilderment as she

1

looked at Doug swaddled in his blanket. After a few seconds, Kathy turned him around so he was facing the same direction as the others. Then she walked to the nurse's station, pulled up a chair, sat down, and typed her user name and password on the computer keyboard. Kathy opened the records for each of the babies and saw that she had typed notes shortly after her shift had begun. But she couldn't remember entering the information, nor could she recall anything else that had happened during her shift, or even what she had done earlier in the day. She was mystified by the memory lapse. Had she gotten sick and blacked out? Did she have a stroke? A stroke would have been crazy; she was only twenty-nine and a marathon runner for God's sake! She gave herself a quick exam to see if there was any evidence of some mishap, perhaps a fall. Her pulse was about 60—normal for her, a long-distance runner. She looked at her arms and hands—there were no bumps, scrapes or bruises. She ran her hands through her short black hair but didn't feel anything unusual; her scalp was smooth and dry. She rubbed her hands over her legs and torso but found nothing unusual. Whatever had happened, she felt lucky that she had woken up in the back of the unit, out of the range of the security camera. But how had she ended up there? Amy, the other nurse on duty, had probably been across the hall during the duration of the strange episode—in the supply room taking inventory or talking to her boyfriend stationed in Iraq—and apparently hadn't noticed her asleep.

Kathy considered making a doctor's appointment to investigate the blackout. But doing so would undoubtedly lead to all kinds of tests, which she had no desire to go through, especially given that her doctor worked out of Polk County Hospital. She would have a tough time keeping the visits and tests confidential.

No one else in the hospital had noticed anything unusual the morning that Kathy blacked out, with the exception of Dudley, the lead third-shift security guard. The security video cameras had gone down for about three minutes, but for much of that time he was distracted, trying to beat his personal record on *Tetris*. He was often hypnotized for hours by the computer game's endless falling tiles. The system came back online only fifteen seconds after he noticed the cameras had gone dark. The outage appeared to be so brief that he never reported it to anyone.

Later that morning, a farmer in Dallas County, which bordered the western edge of West Des Moines, reported that an oval-shaped area in his cornfield, about seventy yards in diameter, had been matted down. In the only local television story about the phenomenon, the reporter called it "just another lonely Iowa farmer looking for attention until harvest."

Four days later, after running fourteen miles effortlessly in preparation for a fall marathon, Kathy Downs completely dismissed the idea of getting a doctor's exam. In the coming years, she occasionally wondered about the night she passed out but never worried about it. She chocked it up to some sort of vagal event. Kathy never passed out again.

Chapter 2

Dr. Ted Strong had delivered difficult news to hundreds of parents during his twenty-five-year career as a clinical researcher for rare retinal diseases. He made sure to use words like "normal" and "happy" when telling them the prognosis for their child, who was blind or soon would be. He'd pick up the plastic model of the human eye off his desk and give a quick lesson in ocular anatomy, explaining how the retina, the thin piece of tissue lining the back of the eye, worked like film or digital sensors in a camera. Retinal cells called rods and cones converted light into electrical signals, which were sent over the optic nerve to the back of the brain to create images. Then he'd explain that a mutation—a misspelling in their child's genetic code—was causing the retinal degeneration and vision loss.

To end these discussions on a hopeful note, Dr. Strong extolled the promises of cutting-edge research that he and his colleagues at the University of Iowa, and other prominent institutions around the world, were conducting. "With emerging gene therapies, we'll soon be able to correct the genetic defect. Someday, we'll be able to grow and transplant new retinas. We will cure these diseases. I have no doubt that within the next decade or so, we will restore your child's vision."

A former power forward and linebacker for the Hawkeyes, Dr. Strong's hulking presence amid his stacks of journals and two computer monitors on his desk left no doubt to the families that he knew what he was talking about, that a cure was within reach.

But on this August day in 1996, as he met with Peter and Peg Anderson, an insurance actuary and his wife, Dr. Strong struggled with describing what he saw—or didn't see—when he looked into their infant's eyes. "Usually, there's *some* atrophy or dysplasia of the rods or cones. We often see pigmentary changes," he said, rubbing his hand through his thinning brown hair. "But with your son, I mean, well, there's hardly any retina. It's so thin, a shadow of what it should be. Yet, the rest of his eyes appear to be relatively normal. The way eye development works, this can't... uh... this shouldn't happen."

Dr. Strong was mystified. He had performed a cursory database search of published research papers but found no reports of any case like it. He had contacted other retinal research colleagues in the United States and Europe, but no one had seen or heard of such a patient. While it might make an intriguing research project for a postdoc, the pursuit of answers to this lone case of virtually nonexistent retinas would likely take the investigator down a rabbit hole—a commitment of thousands of lab hours and vast resources leading to no answers.

Just three months old, Doug Anderson snoozed quietly in his baby carrier on the floor between his parents as Dr. Strong discussed what was wrong with his eyes.

The Andersons looked at each other momentarily and then turned to Dr. Strong. "We understand that our son is blind. We get that," Peter said, glancing back at his wife as he pushed his small, round wire-rimmed glasses higher up the bridge of his nose. "But you've never seen this retinal condition before? Really? *Never?*"

Leaning forward with his elbows on his desk, Dr. Strong exhaled slowly. "Look. In all other respects, your child appears to be perfectly normal. We haven't gotten all the test results back yet, but to my knowledge, no one has ever reported a child being born with such underdeveloped retinas in otherwise normal eyes."

Peg frowned and shook her head. "So why did this happen? Honestly, it is a little scary to hear that our child has something that no one else has ever had. It's really frightening. We can hardly wrap our heads around him being blind."

"I understand your concern, but there's no easy answer. Your son might have a very rare genetic defect. It could have been some type of spontaneous mutation during early development, or it could be inherited. Maybe something happened while you were pregnant. But you said the pregnancy was normal, that there were no accidents or illnesses." Dr. Strong looked down as he shrugged his shoulders. "So... I'm sorry. I just don't know."

"So what does that mean?" Peter asked, trying to understand what the future held for his son.

Dr. Strong glanced back and forth at the Andersons, noticing how similar they looked—both were diminutive with thin light-brown hair, brown eyes, and prominent cheek bones and chins. He thought perhaps they had a common Scandinavian ancestor a few generations back from whom they both inherited the same rare recessive mutation that they passed on to their son, causing his blindness. However, he was reluctant to invest the money and resources to try to identify such a rare mutation. The odds of finding it were stacked against him. And even if he did, gene therapy doesn't help malformed retinas. Something like a retinal transplant would not likely be feasible for decades. Nothing in the foreseeable future would give this child vision.

"Well, while your child's case is unusual, he'll grow up like any other child with vision impairment," he said encouragingly. "I'm not saying it will always be easy. He'll need accommodations. But there are a lot of great resources and technologies out there, and they're getting better every day. He should be OK. And I hope you bring him in every year or two, just so I can make sure there are no further issues or complications."

Little Doug Anderson continued to slumber as the Andersons made the 115-mile journey in their minivan from Iowa City to their home in Des Moines, passing endless rows of tall, late-summer corn. As Peg gazed at the vast fields from the passenger seat, she teared up at the thought of her son never seeing the lush, gently rolling landscape—the leafy green stalks against the deep-blue sky. She also wondered if she and Peter should consider having other children, if they were at risk of having another with this horrible eye condition. Peter rubbed her knee to comfort her but didn't say anything. He was just happy the doctors hadn't found anything else wrong with their son, that Doug didn't have some dreaded terminal disease or an inoperable brain tumor.

In the coming months, the Andersons were pleased with Doug's pleasant disposition. Their son continued to be a good sleeper and rarely cried. Even when he did get cranky, a little music from virtually any station on the radio quickly calmed him down.

In November he began to smile and laugh. All kinds of sounds were mesmerizing to him. He loved to be in the kitchen to listen to the sloshing of the dishwasher and the whir and ding of the microwave. A group of young girls from the neighborhood often came up on the Anderson's porch to visit the happy baby boy. They loved his animated expressions and how he waved and kicked in delight as they sang and cooed to him.

At four months old, Doug's light-blue eyes began to turn bright turquoise, often attracting attention. Complete strangers would comment while passing him at the shopping mall or grocery store, unaware that he had no vision. "I've never seen such beautiful aquamarine eyes before," exclaimed one elderly woman at the Food Lion checkout. "They look like the Caribbean Sea!"

While Peg and Peter appreciated the compliments, they were a reminder that their son was not like other children. In fact, because no one in their families had blue eyes, they figured that Doug's unique eye color directly related to his condition. Why else would his eyes look so different?

Chapter 3

Ziglo's supervisor had assured him that his first assignment—retrieving an adolescent male zing dealer from a path behind the district's commercial sector—would occur without resistance. The Zog wouldn't give the apprentice criminal processor a dangerous or complicated case until he had a few successful arrests under his belt.

This particular suspect was easy to find. He was a repeat offender, usually for zing distribution, and had a location transmitter, a short piece of ultrathin wire, implanted in his rear end. Most low-level zing dealers were harmless youths trying to make money to buy receivers and radios that picked up and archived beloved music transmissions from Earth.

The zow sellers were another story. They were dangerous thugs conducting large, complex operations that moved a highly addictive intoxicant able to knock a Zooban on his or her ass for an entire day. Zing, on the other hand, provided a mellow, short-term high. Many on the planet indulged in zing on a daily basis, usually to relax after work, and remained productive citizens. But zow users were often found hiding from the Zog in Zooba's innumerable towering heaps of discarded consumer goods—toys, furniture, household appliances, and electronic devices. They dug small caves and tunnels in the junk for safe shelter. Many zow addicts were simply part of the clutter and waste that had decimated the planet. The mountainous landfills served as burials for the many zow users who starved to death or overdosed.

Occasionally, the addicts would be forever trapped when their makeshift hideaways collapsed on them.

Ziglo was apprehensive about his first retrieval. It needed to go without a hitch; he wanted to make a good first impression with the Zog. The young Zooban male—tall, barrel-chested with a bushy beard and long, dark brown hair—had been lucky to land the relatively well-paying position. Most Zoobans, including his friends and family, were stuck working in loud, poorly ventilated manufacturing facilities for long hours and low wages, operating and maintaining high-capacity robotic production systems. Ziglo didn't want to blow this special opportunity.

When Ziglo located the suspect, who was walking toward an encampment of addicts squatting by a refuse heap, he did exactly as he had been instructed by his supervisor. He pulled out the disabling wand from the top pocket of his new dark-gray robe, retracted it, and aimed it at the suspect's abdomen. Immediately after he depressed the tiny engagement button with his thumb, the suspect collapsed from the strong pulse of energy emitted by the device. Ziglo was impressed with how effectively it had worked, having never used it on an actual Zooban before. He quickly wrapped the incarceration strap around the suspect's torso and arms before saying or doing anything else. Ziglo felt relieved to find a few small bags of zing vials in the dealer's shoulder satchel. He'd been told that evidence was usually not necessary for efficient processing, but the Zog appreciated it for confirmation of guilt.

The dealer coughed as he struggled to sit up. "This is the third time you guys have caught me. Congratulations. All of Zooba will be so much safer now," he said glibly. His coughing led Ziglo to believe he was one of the young rebellious fools who refused to wear a pollution mask over his nose and mouth. "So are they going to lock me up in the Zohag or just *interrogate* me?"

"Well, we're going there, but I can't say whether they'll keep you. My job is just to retrieve you," Ziglo replied. "Sorry I don't have more information." Ziglo momentarily felt angry at himself for apologizing. He felt he should be tougher, more stoic.

To get to the Zohag, Ziglo and his suspect had to walk past several of the planet's poorly regulated factories—sprawling, five- and six-level windowless buildings that worked to capacity every hour of every day, producing toxic gasses and gigatons of solid waste. They also passed a massive oxygen-filtering dome, emitting loud pulsating roars in its futile effort to remove filth from the air. These structures were built in urban areas with the worst smog but didn't have the capacity to make a significant difference in pollution removal. They were too little, too late in Zooba's effort to clean itself up.

After years of poorly controlled waste production due to hyperconsumption, many of Zooba's seas and waterways were dead. Much of the land had been deforested. Most uninhabited areas were barren and dry, covered in a black powdery residue from the burning of zool, an abundant sedimentary rock used by virtually all of Zooba's manufacturing and power operations.

Shopping was the favorite pastime of virtually all Zoobans—a habit instilled by leaders for their own profit and to distract the citizens from seeking representation in the government. Even when the environmental problems became serious, the planet's leaders could not muster the political will to manage the waste and implement recycling and pollution controls. Most Zooban scientists believed the planet was on the brink of an environmental collapse. Many believed it had reached a point of no return.

As Ziglo and his retrieval passed by a few low-rise, open-air store fronts, "Hit the Road Jack," a favorite Earth song of the Zoobans, blared from an overhead sound system. The iconic rhythm and blues song by Ray Charles had become the de facto anthem for the planned Earth invasion and occupation. Zoobans also had a special affection for Earth musicians who had no vision, because Zoobans themselves had no eyesight.

Thanks to the Zog's well-organized and persistent propaganda machine, all Zoobans knew about the planned Earth takeover, though the timing wasn't yet determined. Citizens were strongly encouraged to learn

11

and speak English, so they could communicate and function well with many of Earth's inhabitants when the time came for occupation. But Ziglo, during his training, had overheard two senior Zog officials discussing a recent successful "Earthling-Zooban baby swap" to see how a Zooban fared on Earth's air, water, and food supply. The officials also mentioned that Zooban scientists were planning to study the retrieved Earthling baby, hoping to figure out how to bestow eyesight to their citizenry.

Ziglo felt a wave of sadness as he and his retrieval approached the Zohag. It didn't make sense to him to be rounding up all these harmless chemical users when the planet was in such a dire predicament. Couldn't the Zog do something more productive or benevolent with its time and resources? But, then again, the planet's situation seemed hopeless. For now, Ziglo felt best to just go with the flow and be thankful he had a decent job. What else could he do? He was just one Zooban.

Ziglo brought the young zing proprietor to a processing room inside the front of the Zohag, a campus of two-dozen tall buildings covered in a dark layer of soot, most of which were overcrowded with criminals. One of the processing officers thanked Ziglo and asked him to sit outside the room in case they had any questions for him during the interrogation.

A few moments later, Ziglo heard his suspect say to him, "See you later. Thanks for a fun time," as he walked quickly toward the exit.

Ziglo panicked, fearing that he'd mishandled the retrieval process, forcing the Zog to let the dealer go. But the processing officer came over and patted Ziglo on the shoulder while giving him back his incarceration strap. "Good job, Zig. Not bad for your first retrieval," he said. "That was really just a test run. Trust me, they won't all be this easy."

Chapter 4

For their son's first-ever show-and-tell assignment in the second grade, Doug's parents encouraged him to talk to the class about his navigational cane as they ate breakfast around a small oval table in the sun-bathed kitchen of their bungalow. "It will help the other kids understand what it's like to be blind, honey," his mom said, resting her hand on his shoulder as she set down a plate with two slices of buttered wheat toast in front of him. "Maybe they'll stop making fun of you for using it... that is, when you do use it."

"Yeah, Doug," his dad said, sitting across from his son. "I know you can get around the house and the school without the cane. But in a big city or an airport or something, man, you're going to wish you knew how to use it better."

Doug frowned as he picked up a slice of toast. "All they're gonna do is laugh and pull on it. They're such jerks."

"Now come on, honey. Mrs. Beasley agreed with us. She thinks if the other kids understand your situation better, your blindness, they'll behave better. She also thinks they're jealous because you're so smart," his mom replied as she pulled up a chair and sat down.

His dad chuckled. "Yeah, you're the brightest kid in the class. I think they're a little intimidated that the blind kid is smarter than they are."

Doug knew his dad was right. No one in the second grade came close to matching his academic skills, especially his ability to memorize facts, figures, sounds, and voices. Also, he amazed people with his adeptness at getting around the school and his neighborhood, often without his cane.

Although he didn't know it, this ability was all thanks to zill—the Zooban radarlike sense that enabled him to sense energy fields and nearby objects through his skin. He still had to be careful near fast-moving objects like cars, bicycles, and a thrown baseball. And, yes, it was frustrating for him to not be able to play games like kickball and hide-and-seek—the favorite recreational activities of his classmates. But in the classroom, he was in his element.

Doug always knew he was different because of his blindness and comments, especially from women, about his beautiful aquamarine eyes. But he'd managed the reality of having no eyesight relatively well and never imagined for a moment that he wasn't human.

Mrs. Beasley shook her head as Doug walked to the front of the class for show-and-tell, holding his cane like a stick he'd found in the woods. Never once did it touch the ground. She continued to look on with disappointment as Doug told the class why he had the cane—how it helped him "avoid bumping into stuff" when he walked.

"Doug, this isn't just 'tell,' it's 'show-and-tell,' so show the class how the navigational cane is used," she said. A short, pudgy woman with thick-framed glasses and an ample bosom, Laura Beasley had endured teasing and bullying since junior high. "Busty Beasley" she'd been called from adolescence into college. As an elementary school teacher for the last ten years, she'd heard plenty of giggling and comments about her "boobies." But she'd learned to brush off the remarks. A reaction or reprimand from her would only embolden the kids.

Doug sighed and began tapping the cane on the floor in front of him as he quickly walked across the front of the classroom. Then he turned around and went back in the other direction. "So that's it. That's how you're supposed to use it," he said after stopping. Pursing his lips, he glanced in the direction of the teacher as if to say, "Now that you've completely embarrassed me, can I go hide under my desk for the rest of the day?"

Mrs. Beasley rolled her eyes slightly. "OK, Doug. Thank you." She decided not to give him any more grief about his lackluster presentation because the wiry blind kid with a mop of wavy brown hair and gorgeous, glowing eyes was, after all, her best student. Maybe it had been too much to ask—to draw attention to his disability.

"So, any questions for Doug?" she asked from the back of the classroom. A few of the kids turned around at their desks and looked back as she spoke. "Don't forget to raise your hand, and I'll call on you."

"So why are you blind? Were you born that way?" blurted out Jeremy Jacobson from the right corner of the back row. He was one of the cane pullers that Doug had complained about, and he had also been reprimanded multiple times during the year for hitting and inappropriate touching of other kids. During one recess earlier in the year, he had tried unsuccessfully to peddle the pills he was taking for ADHD.

Mrs. Beasley pursed her lips. "Jeremy, what did I just say? You raise your hand, mister."

Jeremy lifted his arm with a sheepish grin. "So, uh, why can't you see?"

"That's better. Now that Mr. Jacobson has asked his question appropriately, can you please answer, Doug?"

Turning in Jeremy's direction, Doug said, "Uh-huh. See, I was born with hardly any retinas. It's part of your eye. In the back. You can't see without them." Unconsciously, Doug began tapping his cane on the ground.

The class went silent for a few moments before Mrs. Beasley asked if there were any further questions. No hands went up. The teacher sensed that the class was intimidated by Doug's answer. Not only did the kids not know what retinas were, they didn't appear to have any interest in asking more questions to find it out. The fact that people couldn't see without functioning retinas was all they felt they needed to know.

Later that afternoon, as Doug sat on a swing at recess listening to the ruckus of the other kids from his class playing dodgeball, Jeremy called out to him from across the playground, "Hey Retina Boy, where's your cane?" Everyone heard the barb, including Mrs. Beasley. A few kids laughed. The teacher decided to let it go to see how Doug would handle Jeremy's antagonism.

Jeremy's quip didn't bother Doug all that much. In fact, he took a liking to it as did his classmates. "Retina Boy" stuck as a nickname. It sounded like a moniker for a superhero rather than a label given to someone who didn't quite add up. In the coming weeks, it elevated him in a way, giving him more respect from the other kids. No one, including Doug, had been completely comfortable with his blindness, but the name gave it some appeal and made it easier for everyone to accept him.

His status among his peers got another boost later in the year when the school supplied him with new talking software for his computer, a braille notetaker, and a handheld scanner to read printed materials. There was no need for show-and-tell to explain what these technologies did. His classmates marveled at his high-tech gadgetry, and Retina Boy was glad to demonstrate how it all worked. Mrs. Beasley delighted in the attention that he and his technology drew. It was as if she had her own little Steve Jobs in her classroom.

Chapter 5

As the human Doug Anderson—the real Doug Anderson—lay on a table in a dark, cold research room, he wondered why the Zooban doctors were taking so long to begin their round of daily experiments on him. Usually, by this time several of the researchers were chattering and milling about as they prepared for the tests. He would hear myriad beeps and buzzes of the various machines, and the whooshes of the sliding door as the scientists came and went from the room. They'd place wireless circular probes—only five or ten millimeters in diameter—on his face and forehead, and sometime, on the back of his skull where they had shaved off swaths of hair to expose skin for placement of the monitoring devices. Sometimes they would numb one of his eyes with drops and place the tip of an instrument on it for ten or twenty seconds. Occasionally they'd prick him with a needle—stick it in an arm, hip, or upper leg—to draw blood or take tissue samples.

It was also strange that they hadn't fed him a full breakfast, and instead had given him a chalky, mildly sweet, liquid concoction he'd never had before. His protruding belly gurgled. He was hungry and becoming agitated.

Eventually, he heard the door slide open and guessed that two or three scientists had entered the room. The room was so dark, as it always was, he could never be sure how many scientists were there or exactly what they were doing. Doug couldn't see anything. Occasionally, he'd notice a small orange-yellow flash on the ceiling above him, just beyond the foot of the table—brief surges from a ventilation hole in a small box, a power-system repeater—but they weren't bright enough to illuminate anything or anyone. A few minutes after the scientists arrived, he heard the thud and clank of objects being placed on some type of surface, perhaps a small table, behind his head. Then someone touched his left forearm softly as a small tube emitting a stream of air was placed an inch or so inside of his left nostril. Doug felt a sudden lightness—he felt like he was floating away—but he would never recall the moment they put him under.

Since Doug's arrival on Zooba, the scientists had been studying him from head to toe: his brain and eyes, neurological functions, internal organs, and musculoskeletal system. The data gleaned from the tests were analyzed by sophisticated computers. It didn't take long for the Zooban scientists to figure out that except for having functional retinas, humans were strikingly similar to the Zooban species. Over time, the scientists focused more on Doug's eyes and retinas. Understanding how eyesight worked became their singular goal.

Doug lived in a small apartment adjacent to the laboratory. Each room—the living area, kitchen, and bathroom—had a narrow rectangular window to let in ambient light. A few dimly glowing tubes ran across the ceiling in each room to provide him with some illumination at night. They brought in a nutritionist once a week to ensure that the Zooban diet was keeping him healthy. Like many Zooban youth, he was taught both the Zooban and English languages, the latter of which would be helpful in the planned Earth takeover, if they decided to use him as a negotiating or diplomatic resource. After all, he was human. Maybe Earthlings would respond well to him.

For the first few years of his life, Doug had enjoyed the attention pored upon him from all the adults. He knew he was special because he could see with his eyes, and propaganda about him, the special child from Earth, had filled the Zooban airwaves. But without having exposure to other children, Zooban or human, he hadn't learned how to interact appropriately with others and became upset when the focus wasn't on him. He was prone to tantrums and outbursts when he didn't get what he wanted. When he reached the age of eight, the scientists felt they had collected much of the information they needed on Doug. As a result, the professionals who cared for him in the apartment were replaced by unskilled transient workers just looking for easy income. They took very little interest in him, which only exacerbated his depression and bad behavior.

With more unoccupied time on his hands, Doug began wondering about Earth. He wondered what it would be like to walk around a place where everyone else was sighted like he was, and the air and water were so clean. What would a planet without pollution riddling its land and air look like? What would *he* look like to everyone else? What would it be like not to be different?

Based on the intercepted broadcasts from Earth he heard over the Zooban airwaves, it seemed to Doug that humans were happy and ener-getic, more so than Zoobans. They were always playing music and games in large stadiums and concert halls. They were always driving around in the fast, powerful vehicles he heard so much about on commercials. Human food and drinks—cold Buds, refreshing Cokes, and juicy Double Whoppers—made everyone feel so good. The planet even had food called Happy Meals!

But during his loneliest moments, Doug wondered if his parents back on Earth even knew he existed. Doug knew he'd been swapped for a Zooban child, but did his real mother and father have any idea that the child they had in their home wasn't human? Maybe they would, because the boy would be blind. But would his mom and dad love their strange son, or would they have discarded him as some freak? He also wondered if the Zooban kid had any idea that he was an alien.

Doug had difficulty imagining what would happen if he were someday able to go back to Earth to be with his real parents. He couldn't picture what they looked like or how they would react to learning that he was their real son. Would they be happy and embrace him or just shake their heads and turn away in disappointment? Regardless, he felt in his heart he would never find out. Earth for Doug seemed to be only a dream.

When Doug awakened, the left side of his face was numb. The sensation wasn't completely unfamiliar—he'd received local anesthetics for biopsies in which the scientists took small punches of skin—but this numbness covered a much larger area.

After he regained much of his consciousness, a young female research assistant escorted him down the short path back to his apartment. She was shorter than most adult Zoobans—not much taller than Doug—but had their characteristic long brown hair and bulky torso. Her gray robe was cleaner than most that others wore. She knew what the scientists had done to Doug that morning but was instructed not to say anything to him about the procedure. Neither she nor Doug spoke while they walked, though he could tell that something was covering the left side of his face because of his obscured field of vision. He walked slowly, still feeling the effects of the anesthesia. The assistant stopped frequently, enabling him to catch up.

Doug noticed a frown on the young Zooban's face as they took the elevator to the fifth floor. When they arrived at his apartment door, she said, "They want you to rest today. Don't do anything too strenuous. In a day or two, they'll remove the patch." She touched his forearm with her hand before she turned and walked away.

Doug had become a big fan of American football. The Zooban authorities provided him with transmitters—small rectangular cards with wireless buds that adhered to ear lobes—which contained entire seasons of National Football League radio broadcasts. With more time on his hands, as the frequency of experiments and educational lessons diminished, he listened to more and more football. On the evening after his procedure, as he listened to a dramatic game between the Washington Redskins and Dallas

Cowboys, he had a difficult time focusing on the action. As he lay in bed, he ran his fingers across the smooth surface of the soft patch that covered the left side of his face. He wasn't in pain or discomfort, but something about his face felt different. He knew they had done something to his eye.

Two days later, when the scientists removed the patch, Doug's field of vision on his left remained completely obscured. They didn't say anything more about the procedure, only that he could return to normal activities, and there likely wouldn't be any further tests for a long time. When he returned to his apartment, he immediately went into the kitchen, the room with the strongest illumination, and looked at himself in the shiny surface of a wall that he used as a makeshift mirror. His saw that his left eye was gone, replaced by a smooth piece of synthetic skin slightly darker than the surrounding skin. Except for the color difference, there was virtually no evidence that an eye, or even a socket for it, had ever been there. Doug gasped at the sight of himself. He was horrified and felt utterly helpless; there was no one on Zooba who could understand the humiliation he felt from his disfigurement.

The rest of that day and night Doug lay curled up in a fetal position on his couch, sometimes crying in grief, other times overwhelmed by the fear that they'd take his other eye. Not only did he know that he would never be able to manage blindness as easily as Zoobans managed theirs, he knew that vision was what made him special. Without vision, he'd be nothing.

The next afternoon, another new caretaker arrived. She was a teenager—much younger than any of her predecessors—and uncharacteristically thin with long red hair. "Hello, Doug!" she said as if giving a proclamation when he engaged the sliding front door to let her in. "So you are the famous human boy! Wow! Well, I'm Zellie. I'll be taking care of you until tomorrow morning." Doug looked at her suspiciously, wondering what was behind her ebullience; he couldn't believe she was so excited to take care of him, the rejected Earthling. Zellie immediately sensed negative energy, perhaps dysfunction, in the living area. She could tell something was wrong, especially when he didn't reply to her friendly introduction. She quickly checked out the other rooms to make sure there were no surprising smells like rotting food or a plop of feces, the trademarks of other neglected Zooban kids she'd cared for.

Doug, sitting on his couch, looked up at Zellie as she returned from her inspection of the other rooms. She was smiling, relieved to have not found any messes. Something about Zellie was different from his other caregivers. She had a brightness, a glow. Her eyes were glassy, almost shimmering. And she seemed genuinely happy to be with Doug. He felt safe with her.

"Two days ago, they took out one of my eyes," he said, looking down at the floor, his voice quivering. "They didn't even tell me. They just did it. I woke up and it was gone. My left eye." Doug looked up at Zellie to see her reaction. Tears were running down his cheek.

Zellie had been told about the enucleation when she signed up for Doug's case. She still couldn't imagine what it would be like to have an eye removed, especially if she were human and used her eyes for that incredible sense known as vision. "Whoa. Can you still see? I mean, with one eye?"

"Yeah," he replied. Then he began to sob as Zellie sat down next to him, frozen in thought. She knew the scientists had lost interest in the young human. They wouldn't have had someone as inconsequential as her take care of him had they wanted to continue their experiments. He was now disposable, and the removal of his eye was incontrovertible evidence of that fact.

Zellie herself had been cast off by Zooban society after her parents were killed in a factory explosion. She was about Doug's age when the tragedy occurred and had spent most of the last few years providing care for orphans and troubled youth. It was difficult, thankless work given only to those for whom there was no future—or at least no future that had been planned. But an orphan herself, she empathized with the young lost souls and tried to be as caring and compassionate as she could.

After a few minutes, as Doug's crying diminished to a whimper, Zellie pulled a small vial of pink powder out of her satchel. She poured a tiny amount into the cap and handed it to him. "This stuff is called zing. Just put it on your tongue. It'll make you feel better," she said reassuringly. "It's about time you got zinged."

Zellie had thought for a moment about the ramifications of giving the intoxicant to Doug. He was so young. Another hit or two, and he'd likely be hooked on it. But there were chemicals far more powerful and addictive that were widely used in their district, and maybe a steady zing habit would keep him from venturing down a more destructive path. After all, he had no future. Why not enable him to enjoy the few pleasures available to him? He needed an escape.

Doug took the cap from Zellie and turned over the contents on his outstretched tongue. Within a minute he began to feel a warm, tingling sensation throughout his body, especially in his limbs. He felt lighter, almost weightless. He looked into Zellie's blue-green eyes. How beautiful Zellie suddenly became to him. All the bad feelings, even the horror of having lost an eye, melted away.

The high lasted only twenty minutes, and he'd learn later that he'd have to wait a few hours before his body and mind would recalibrate to feel the effects of another dose. But this was the best he'd ever felt in his young, inconceivable life.

Chapter 6

Peter and Peg Anderson were conflicted about letting their son explore the neighborhood alone during summer evenings after dinner. On one hand, they were thrilled that he wasn't glued to the radio and was instead communing with nature and getting exercise. On the other hand, it seemed irresponsible to let their blind ten-year-old roam freely, as far as three or four miles from their home. They imagined rabid pedophile rapists with cleavers and machetes lurking in the backyards, parks, and playgrounds of Des Moines. And even though they knew that virtually no violent crimes had been reported in the community, what would the neighbors think of the Andersons if something by chance *did* happen to their *blind* child, who had been left alone and unsupervised? They knew he had a navigational gift and could avoid many dangers, but an accident could happen to anyone. If something untoward did happen to their blind boy, the ridicule would certainly be endless.

Retina Boy would occasionally walk for a couple of miles down a heavily wooded trail that ran through the park behind their house. Underneath a canopy of maples, elms, and firs, the dirt path was cool and serene. He felt energized by the thick and fragrant air, especially after it rained. He often marveled at the chirping, warbling, and other calls and responses of the myriad birds that inhabited their sanctuary. Sometimes he would stop on the path and listen, trying to figure out who was talking to whom and what their conversation might be about. Perhaps they were sending out warnings to one another about him, the intruder. Or maybe they knew he was harmless because he was blind, and they were letting one another know he was not a danger.

Retina Boy's favorite excursion was a paved, often-secluded path on the perimeter of the park that stretched for a couple of miles between a thick meadow and a cornfield. A steady wind frequently came out of the west across the field of waist-high grass and wildflowers. On the other side of the path, he could hear the rustling of cornstalk leaves, which became louder over the summer as the plants grew taller, well above his head. He relished spending time in the wide-open landscape, away from the activity and noise in his suburban neighborhood. Most of all, he loved the soothing, rhythmic chirp of the crickets at dusk during the latter half of summer.

One evening in late September as Retina Boy was returning from an after-dinner stroll through the neighborhood, a girl called out "hello" to him from the porch of a two-story bungalow. When Retina Boy turned around, she immediately knew he was blind because he didn't make direct eye contact.

"Hey," he replied, surprised that he hadn't sensed her presence before she spoke. "My name is Doug. "I live down the street. Most people call me Retina Boy because I'm blind." He was never shy about being blind. He found it easier to put that information out right away so people would understand that he couldn't see them.

"I'm Marcy," she replied, relieved that the boy was friendly and forth-coming. "I'm sort of new to the neighborhood, so I don't know many kids." Marcy thought about telling him that she was in a wheelchair because of a spinal cord injury. She thought about launching into the whole story about the jungle gym fall when she was five years old, but just couldn't muster the courage to get it out. For once, her chair was invisible to someone. "Is it hard being blind?" she decided to ask her new acquaintance. "Do other kids make fun of you?"

"Well, they do sometimes," he replied. "But they also make fun of me because I'm pretty smart. I mean, I do really well in school. Sometimes I'm not sure if they think I'm weird or if they're just jealous. I wish I could play sports. I really love baseball, but I just listen to it on the radio."

Marcy felt a wave of relief, almost a rush, in having met someone who was different like she was. Also, like her, he seemed honest and smart. As she felt more trusting of him, she talked about her wheelchair and also about her classes in school and favorite internet sites. They both happened to be in the fifth grade but didn't share any classes. They exchanged email addresses, and Marcy promised to send him information about a new cell phone she had just gotten for her birthday. Her only disappointment was that he couldn't see her coveted moon-landing T-shirt, with an image of Neil Armstrong taking his first iconic step. Nor could he see her beautiful bushy curls that drew frequent compliments, even from people who had known her for some time.

A few days later, during morning school announcements, Retina Boy heard that Marcy had won the fifth-grade spelling bee. Impressed, he decided to go back to her house to see if she would be around. She never sent him an email as she had promised, but that didn't deter him from trying to find out more about the talkative, brainy girl in his neighborhood. Sure enough, she was there on her porch when he went back down her street the following week.

Marcy couldn't believe that Retina Boy—or any kid for that matter—had made the effort to seek her out. Even though they had seemed to hit it off when they met, she was convinced she'd never see him again. But there he was on the sidewalk in front of her house, nervously running his hand through his brown mop of hair, looking in her direction with his beautiful aquamarine eyes and shy half smile.

"So, I heard you won the spelling bee," he said. "That's pretty cool. What word did you win on?"

Marcy blushed. "Well, I won on 'innocuous.' It really was an easy word, but the other kid forgot the second *u*."

Retina Boy grinned. "I probably would have messed it up, too."

"I'm gonna need to study more," Marcy continued, "for the state competition later in the year."

"That's really cool," replied Retina Boy, nodding and smiling.

"Look, if you want to come up on the porch and hang out for a little bit, that would be OK," Marcy said, surprised by her courage to invite him up.

"Sure, OK."

Marcy watched in amazement as her new friend, who was supposedly blind, slowly stepped over to and straight up the concrete walkway that bisected the lawn of Marcy's house. When he arrived at the seven steps leading up to the porch, he paused for a second before climbing them at a measured pace but without hesitation.

Marcy gasped. "How did you do that?"

"Do what?" answered Retina Boy.

Marcy shook her head. "Never mind, it's OK."

Marcy and Retina Boy quickly became best buddies, hanging out on her porch and going for excursions around the neighborhood and along his favorite paths. Practically speaking, Marcy and he were a perfect pair. She was his eyes, and he was her legs. Retina Boy loved to wheel her around while they talked about school and how well they did in classes. On rainy days, they would sit on Marcy's porch and listen to the countless tiny droplets of water crashing to the earth and the thunder rolling in the distance. Retina Boy loved storms and hearing the tornado siren go off when severe weather was approaching.

And Retina Boy grew to like Marcy very much. Never before had he met another kid so smart or so obsessed with history and knowledge. She knew all about wars and presidents and was especially fascinated by space travel. Marcy loved to tell Retina Boy stories, and to his amazement, he loved to listen. She knew all about the Apollo missions and the first moon landing, which he found particularly intriguing. He delighted in hearing Marcy talk about the astronauts and their adventures.

"If I could choose to see one thing, it would be the stars in the sky," he said to her one afternoon while they were hanging out on her porch.

"If I could do one thing, it would be to go on a spacewalk," Marcy replied. "Wouldn't it be so cool to float around weightless and look at Earth and all the stars? I wouldn't even need a wheelchair!"

"Well, that sounds sort of scary. I mean being in space," Retina Boy said, looking down and shrugging his shoulders. "I'd probably pee in my space pants."

Chapter 7

The extreme snow, ice, cold, and wind of the long Iowa winters were tough on most everyone, but especially on Marcy and Retina Boy. It was hard to navigate a wheelchair, even on a shoveled sidewalk, and many of Retina Boy's favorite walking routes weren't cleared. And if they were, sometimes it was just too blustery to spend any meaningful time outdoors. So, they hung out at each other's houses after school and on the weekends.

They could often be found in Retina Boy's basement, which was the home of his dad's collection of more than a thousand vinyl records. Much of it was folk and rock from the 1960s and 1970s, but there was a shelf of about sixty-five ambient and electronica records, many of the same vintage. These were Retina Boy's favorites, and his father had put braille labels on the covers so he could identify them. He loved Tangerine Dream, the German electronic group known for its explorative, atmospheric soundtracks, and Brian Eno, known for entrancing, minimalistic tape loops, a technique used on his album *Music for Airports*. Retina Boy surmised that the short, repetitive ascending and descending phrases on some of the album's tracks—just six or seven soft, resonant notes from a synthesizer— were sonic metaphors for the takeoff and landing of airplanes.

Most of the albums popped and crackled when they were played because of the abuse they'd gotten during his father's college days. But to Retina Boy, the imperfections gave them character. Contemporary music recordings sounded sterile to him because of their high production quality.

No one else he knew had old vinyl treasures like his dad's, which made them all the more special.

Marcy loved to watch her friend's transfixed gaze—the fascination in his deep aquamarine eyes—as they listened to the spacious, progressive music. It was his tonic, the fuel for his mind. She could see that the music gave his world color and texture.

Marcy knew that Retina Boy would likely never see, or if he did, it wouldn't happen for decades. She'd gone to one appointment at Dr. Strong's office to learn more about his condition. While the doctor said there were treatments emerging for many blinding retinal diseases, building an entirely new retina was another challenge entirely and still well off into the future. Sometimes she felt bad for her friend that he'd never be able to enjoy watching tall trees bending in the wind or gazing into the endless blue of the summer sky. He'd never see her brown eyes, thick blonde curls, or scrunched-up face when she got angry.

But then again, how did Retina Boy know what he was missing? He'd been blind since the day he was born. What would it be like to see for the first time at the age of thirty or forty?

Classmates and kids around the neighborhood often asked him if he longed to see things. He usually replied with a shrug of his shoulders and tried to change the subject. He'd learned how to live pretty well without eyesight and was content being blind. Why shake things up? What if he did get vision someday and didn't like what he saw?

However, he wasn't completely ambivalent about the mysterious sense known as vision, and one afternoon while he was taking Marcy through the park, he asked, "Are there clouds out today? What are they like?"

"Well, there aren't many today. Just a few. Kinda fluffy. Not too big," she answered. "I really didn't notice them all that much. They're just there."

"Yeah. I wonder about clouds a lot. I mean, they're magical to me the way they float in the air, but an airplane can fly right through them. When I was little, my mom said they were like cotton candy. But cotton candy gets your fingers all sticky. So, I don't know. I really wish I could see a cloud, what one really looks like."

Marcy turned around for a moment in her chair to look at Retina Boy. She was surprised by his comments. He didn't talk much about vision or his lack of it. It was one of the few times she felt sad for him—that he couldn't see.

"Cumulonimbus are definitely the coolest clouds. They're the thunderheads that storms are made of. They tower into the sky. Fifty or sixty thousand feet. We learned that in science," Marcy said. "I wish you could see lightning. It's electricity in the sky, positive charges connecting with negative charges. It's really cool." She felt like she could talk for hours, telling Retina Boy what the whole world looked like. But she was afraid to upset him. Marcy turned around again to see his reaction.

Retina Boy was grinning. She had piqued his curiosity, though he didn't ask any more questions. But for years to come, whenever a thunderstorm rolled through, he would remember that conversation and how his great friend marveled at the intense weather. What a beautiful picture she had painted for him. In a way, she was the best eyes he could ever wish for.

Chapter 8

On Zooba, Doug was looking every day at a dark, hazy sky—a blanket of gray with occasional streaks and patches of muted purple. While it orbited a sun much like Earth did, Zooba was dim even during the day because of the shroud of pollution. Zooba had very little precipitation, so the filth was rarely cleared from the air.

Doug spent most days alone in his apartment, waiting for Zellie's arrival in the evenings—Zellie and her zing. He also enjoyed listening to broadcasts and recordings from Earth, which came from audio cards sold by local vendors. He received a small allowance to buy these minor luxuries. Also, they were broadcast by a free planetwide radio system that could be heard in most public areas. While the system carried a variety of music and news, it also included programming from Zooba's political leaders to get the citizens pumped up about the planned Earth invasion and the promise of clean air, clean water, and bounties of lush foliage. One of their slogans was simply "We are going," which caught on with the public, for better or worse. It was often used—both sincerely and facetiously—at the end of a discussion about the environment. Those who disapproved of the planned takeover would say mockingly, "We are going nowhere."

Doug most enjoyed listening to sporting events. He was transfixed by American football announcers delivering the play-by-play with emotion and urgency. While he didn't understand all the rules and penalties, he could follow a game's back and forth flow as the action moved across the field. He loved when an announcer yelled "fumble" or "touchdown," and the crowd erupted in the background. He himself would sometimes jump up from his couch during dramatic moments, even if he wasn't quite sure what was happening on the field. He wondered what it would be like to be at the game and see and hear fifty thousand fans cheering for their team after a big play. How incredible he thought that must be.

Many evenings after partaking in a round of zing, Zellie and Doug would walk through the Zooban commercial zone, a series of interconnected stores—much like American strip malls—selling just about everything imaginable: pollution masks, air-filtering systems, several varieties of talking dolls, radios, audio cards, voice recorders, sound-based electronic games, three-wheeled bicycles, and electric scooters. Some vendors sold small personal horns, each with a unique sound, which Zoobans used to identify each other when separated or in a large crowd. Most everyone had what were essentially cell phones placed on an ear or garment, but the horns were as much recreational as they were practical. The way a Zooban blew his or her horn was like an audio fashion statement. Zellie could make her horn sound like a low-pitched fart when she passed young Zooban males who were rude or trying hard to impress her.

About every one hundred yards was a bakery selling zoofeejee, a small crusted roll with a sweet filling having the consistency of melted cheese. They were made entirely from synthetic ingredients. The delectable aroma of this Zooban staple wafted throughout the commercial district. Each proprietor had their own secret recipe for the filling, which included all sorts of vitamins and nutrients, as well as laxatives and energy boosters. Zoofeejee vendors claimed that one could live off the rolls, and some of the poorer population did, though their skin had an orange tint from high doses of carotenoid-like ingredients.

Navigating the district at night could be challenging for Doug because it was so dark. He had to rely on incidental light emitted by power stations— small box-shaped generators used by most of the vendors. They were usually attached to a wall or ceiling. Fortunately, the Zooban scientists had enough

36

benevolence to put lighting, albeit dim, in his apartment. They also developed a small flashlight-like device so he could get around outdoors at night. But in their haste, they didn't design it well, and its charge lasted only an hour or two.

Day and night, the Zooban marketplace was filled with a cacophony of sounds, including intercepted radio broadcasts from Earth and takeover propaganda, personal horns, and proprietors announcing sales and specials on their goods. A typical Earthling would have had a difficult time picking out individual sources of sounds from the cornucopia of noise, but Zoobans were accustomed to it, and had no problem tuning into different channels of music and waves of chatter.

Doug and Zellie often hung out at a small, out-of-the-way zoofeejee café—it had only seven tables and an open façade—but they loved that it played Earth's rock-and-roll music from the 1970s and 1980s. They could stay there for hours—even do a hit of zing—and no one cared. The vendor's zoofeejee were chewier than most and didn't sell very well. But Doug and Zellie enjoyed tugging on the pastries with their teeth—it made for a more engaging, almost comical, dining experience.

About one hundred feet above the café ran one of the busiest routes of the Zee, a monorail transportation system crisscrossing the planet, primarily connecting commercial sectors. Unlike Earth's subways and trains, the Zee ran long windowless carriages, which held as many as three hundred passengers and ran on a thin power cable above the cars.

The Zee was an expensive ride and was used primarily by the affluent—members of the Zog and merchants who had large commercial franchises. The transport system was well maintained and equipped with a highly efficient climate-control system that not only kept the cabin air clean but also pumped in extra oxygen to relax and refresh its passengers. While it was a favorite place for conducting business, many riders were simply taking time out of their day to get away from the dirt and noise of the crowded Zooban streets. Neither food nor children were permitted on the Zee—rules imposed to maintain a sense of order and tidiness.

While most Zoobans had never ridden the system, the sound of it whizzing by—a "*zeeeeeooooooohhhh*"—was a persistent reminder of the planet's hierarchy. Those with power and wealth could literally speed above the masses.

Doug occasionally stood outside the café to marvel at the long metallic tubes speeding by, wondering if somehow, someday, he could take what surely must be an incredible ride. The Zee was a symbol of adventure and freedom. Doug happened to be the only being on the planet who could watch the Zee zooming by. For him, it was an unattainable escape from his world of isolation and boredom.

One evening when the café had picked up a Detroit station playing a block of pop classics by The Hollies—"Carrie Anne," "Bus Stop," "Long Cool Woman"—Doug asked Zellie a question that had been burning inside him for a long time. He hadn't posed it before because he was afraid of the answer.

"You know, it would be really great if I could make it back to Earth someday," he said. "I mean, I think I'd be happier there. Maybe Earthlings would care about me more. I'm one of them after all. Do you think I'll ever go?"

Zellie looked down to hide her sad expression from her friend who might see it with his eye. She had had a tough life, but she couldn't imagine how difficult it was for Doug who had been abducted, disfigured, and discarded.

"Well, if you do go make sure you take me with you," she said, looking up, trying to be encouraging. "It would be great just to breathe some clean air, you know?"

Doug nodded. "Yeah, it would be."

While he and Zellie sat silently, a Hollies tune, now iconic on Zooba, played through the speaker in the ceiling above their table.

> Sometimes, all I need is the air that I breathe
> And to love you
> All I need is the air that I breathe

Doug and Zellie smiled broadly. The synchronicity was a hopeful sign, as if someone or something out there were looking after them. "Zellie, you're my only friend. I don't see how I could make it without you," Doug said. They were the nicest words his Zooban companion had ever heard.

Chapter 9

Marcy was pissed. She sat in the back of her mom's van with her arms folded and a sneer on her face. They were on their way to the Hawkeye Music Machine to pick up a recorder and lesson book. All summer, Marcy had protested learning a musical instrument. "I'd rather join the stinking track team," she had said to her parents at dinner the previous night.

Along with Retina Boy, she was one of the top performing students in the sixth grade—especially in math and science—but her parents insisted that she study some type of art or creative subject.

"Marcy, you need to exercise the right side of your brain," her father had said during dinner. "It'll help you get into a good college down the road."

"I'm eleven, Dad." She had rebutted. "Anyway, when I ace the SATs, I'll be able to go most anywhere I want... as long as they don't care about the chair."

Her argument was solid—she probably would score extremely well on her college entrance exam and be recruited by top universities. But on the recommendation from teachers to be firmer with their brilliant but stubborn little girl and expand her interests beyond math and science, her parents wouldn't back down.

Marcy's mother invited Retina Boy to come with them to the music store in hopes it would defuse the tension. But he just sat quietly next to Marcy in the back, afraid that he'd only make matters worse if he said anything.

Retina Boy waited with Marcy and her mom at the store's front counter while a clerk went into the stockroom to retrieve a few different types of recorders to show them. The store was quiet except for someone in the back strumming chords on an acoustic guitar. The sound was crisp and fresh. Except for a couple of student band concerts at school, Retina Boy hadn't heard much live music. He could feel the sound waves coming from the instrument even though he was standing fifty feet away. The chord changes were swift and smooth; this player had the agility and precision of someone who knew what they were doing. Retina Boy walked to the back of the store to get closer to the source of the strumming.

"Hey," said the player, a young man, as Retina Boy approached. "What's goin' on?"

"Hey," replied Retina Boy. "That sounds pretty good."

Will immediately knew Retina Boy was blind from his unfixed gaze, though he'd never seen anyone with such hypnotic blue-green eyes. He was instantly determined to try to get the kid signed up for lessons. Over the last couple of years, Will had had two students who were blind, and both had near perfect pitch. They were his most talented charges, able to play by ear just about everything he taught them. Ultimately, both went away to college and never came back. Will was stuck teaching unmotivated kids who took lessons because their parents made them. There were also occasional adolescent boys who wanted to be overnight lead guitar sensations but lacked the chops and discipline to become any good. If only his students practiced once in a while.

Though Will had visions of making it big himself—his band had landed some nightclub gigs in Iowa City, Omaha, and Lincoln—the teaching job wasn't a bad way to earn a little money in the short-term. Regardless of what happened with his band, Will would always be part of the music scene. A diminutive young man with a pony tail and wisp of black hair on his chin, he could usually be found at the Hawkeye, a nightclub, or the Drake University radio station, where he hosted a Tuesday and Thursday afternoon show called *Pretzel Logic*. It wasn't often that he didn't have a guitar in his hands.

"Yeah, we just got this mahogany cutaway in... a Martin," said Will as he began to fingerpick lightly. "It's got a deep, warm sound. Good for ballads. You know, the mellow stuff."

"Yeah," said Retina Boy, nodding, though he had no idea what type of wood the instruments were normally made of.

"Do you play?"

"Nah, I've never really tried."

"You should," Will said as he put down the Martin and picked up a black-and-white Stratocaster from a stand behind him. "Who knows, maybe you have some talent."

Retina Boy shrugged his shoulders.

Will plugged a cable into a 100-watt Marshall amp and smiled knowingly as he turned the volume knob clockwise. Then he pressed up and down on a pedal on the floor. Holding all of his fingers across the fretboard, he strummed three measures of a loud but muffled *chunk, achunka chunka chunka chunka, chunk* sound.

Then he lit up the store with a soaring *wah, nah-nah-nah, nah-nah-nah-nah-nah... Wah, nah-nah-nah, nah-nah*. Retina Boy was excited to recognize it right away as the intro to "Voodoo Child (Slight Return)" from the album *Electric Ladyland*. It was in his dad's vinyl collection.

The powerful scream and whine from the guitar amp made the hair on the back of Retina Boy's neck and forearms stand up. He felt a huge jolt of adrenaline. It was as if he'd stuck his finger in a light socket. Though his parents were agnostic—perhaps one could call them secular protestant at most on December 25—he had just found religion.

Will continued the iconic riff for a few more measures as Retina Boy stood frozen in awe, mouth agape. Will knew he was reaching the kid. Then the clerk from the front came over to ask him to stop.

"Uh, Mr. Hendrix," the clerk said holding a recorder in his hand. "I'm trying to explain to the nice ladies the differences between these fine wind instruments, but they may not have any hearing left if you keep it up."

"Oh, sorry dude," said Will, grinning and raising his eyebrows. He looked over at Retina Boy, who was also smiling.

Three days later, Retina Boy was back at the Hawkeye Music Machine with his mom to pick up an acoustic guitar and sign up for lessons with Will. Though Retina Boy had been mesmerized by the electric guitar, Will insisted that he start with an acoustic, which was harder to play but would build up his calluses and finger strength.

Like Will's other blind students, Retina Boy picked up music by ear. Within a few weeks, in addition to memorizing the notes on the upper part of the fretboard, he had learned several basic chords—C, E, Em, F, G, A, Am, D. Playing guitar came to him easily, though he made sure, as Will had instructed, to practice at least an hour a day. Next he learned scales, which gave him the chops he needed to play lead. In two months, he was improvising, playing along with his dad's Neil Young and Bob Dylan records. But Jimmy Page became his hero—Retina Boy aspired to some day match his agility and speed. For hours on end, he practiced the opening to "Black Dog," the first riff Will had taught him.

However, trying to play Jimmy Page leads on an acoustic guitar was difficult and sounded underwhelming—the strings were harder and stiffer than those for an electric guitar— so Retina Boy was back at the Hawkeye Music Machine with his dad to buy the very same black-and-white Stratocaster that he had heard Will play three months earlier.

While Retina Boy was practicing in the basement one evening after dinner, his dad, having coffee with his wife upstairs, said, "Peg, I know this may sound weird—perhaps I'm just a typical proud parent who can't say enough about his kid—but I think Doug might become really good some-day. I mean, like, even a rock star."

"I know, I've been thinking the same thing," Peg said as she carried a plate from the dining room into the kitchen. "It comes to him so naturally. It's a little scary because he's so smart but might follow that kind of shady career path, you know, sex and drugs and rock and roll."

"They're all my brain and body need," Peter said in a British accent, channeling Ian Dury and the Blockheads.

"Well, I hope to God if he does become a rock star, he can write better songs than that."

"Don't worry. He will. He'll write something like 'Stairway to Des Moines.'"

Peg punched Peter in the shoulder as she walked behind him. "You're such a weirdo," she said, shaking her head.

Like the Andersons, Marcy appreciated Retina Boy's musical passion and talent. She loved to watch and listen to him play. However, her music career never got off the ground—literally. The recorder purchased at the Hawkeye was found smashed to pieces in her driveway three days after it was purchased. No one dared ask Marcy how the instrument met its demise.

Chapter 10

"I am pleased to introduce two amazing fourteen-year-olds. They are both at the top of their class, they are talented musicians, and, most important, they are both good, amiable young men. Furthermore, they are helping me and the retinal research community advance our vision-saving projects. Please join me in welcoming Doug Anderson and Danny Pullman."

Dr. Ted Strong had just finished extolling the promise of his research efforts to a crowd of more than two hundred people who had come to Chicago to learn about the latest advances in overcoming inherited retinal diseases. Now he was introducing two likable patients who stood to benefit from his work.

During his keynote address, he told the hopeful donors of the National Retina Research Foundation—people and families affected with inherited retinal diseases, many accompanied by guide dogs and navigational canes—that Danny had been selected to participate in a Phase 2 clinical trial for a gene therapy for people with retinitis pigmentosa caused by mutations in a gene called rhodopsin. "Both Danny and his mom have the mutation in rhodopsin, but given that her phenotype is so mild—that is, she has minimal vision loss—we're going to wait to treat her," he said. "Rhodopsin is a gene expressing a protein that kicks off the biochemical process in the retina—the process that enables us to see. When light hits the back of your eye, rhodopsin gets the visual cycle started. By replacing the defective copies of rhodopsin with healthy copies, we're hopeful we can save and maybe even restore Danny's vision. The early safety study has given us an indication that the treatment works."

Dr. Strong's message for Doug Anderson's case was more difficult to deliver. "Frankly, Doug's case has been quite challenging—it is quite unusual," Dr. Strong said before pulling away from the microphone to clear his throat and consider how he wanted to articulate his lack of success. "But we have hope for giving Doug vision. We are learning how to build new retinas from stem cells, and there's even the development of a bionic vision-enabling device that connects directly to the brain, bypassing the eye entirely."

A few people in the audience oohed and aahed.

"That brain thing sounds kinda creepy," Retina Boy said to Danny as they sat in chairs behind Dr. Strong, waiting to tell their stories to the audience.

"Really, man," Danny replied, nodding in agreement. He, like Retina Boy, was a skinny young teenager with thick brown hair, though he was taller and gangly.

Danny had met Retina Boy the day before at the opening luncheon of the conference. Throughout the meal, the boys were shushed by their parents during speeches and the annual award ceremony honoring volunteers. Danny and Retina Boy had become instant buddies, talking mostly about their favorite classic-rock bands and musicians.

Before the lunch was over, Danny asked Retina Boy to join his fledgling band. The boys lived a few miles from each other, and even though he had never heard Retina Boy play, Danny knew his new pal probably had talent based solely on the songs and riffs he claimed to know. Danny, who had been drumming for almost five years, was the unofficial leader of the band. He decided to give Retina Boy a tryout, and if all went well, he'd take Sammy off lead guitar and just have him sing. Sammy was more interested in showing off the limited talent he had rather than working to get better.

"I think everyone in the band can play OK... sort of. I can hack my way through just about anything—some Zeppelin, Deep Purple, Pearl Jam. We just need to practice and get some real gigs," he told Retina Boy while wolfing down a piece of chocolate cake after lunch. "We have decent bass and keyboards, though Sammy's kind of weak on the guitar. It would be great to get someone who can jam."

After having spent more than a year playing along with records in his basement, this was exactly the opportunity Retina Boy was hoping for. Perhaps playing with a band that wasn't well established would be a good thing, given he'd never played with anyone else before. He felt he still had a lot of learning to do. He wanted to play better, and the band would be a great way to take his skills to the next level.

After the lunch program ended, Danny had one burning question left for Retina Boy. "Sounds like you know a lot of tunes and riffs, which is great," said Danny. "But if you're completely blind and always have been, how do you learn the music?"

"I learn it by ear, and then I practice it a lot."

"Seriously? You don't read music?"

"Not really. I mean, I know the notes and chords when I hear them. I have this great guitar teacher, this guy, Will, who helps me. He's trying to get me to use a metronome and not rush through stuff. But Will's really cool."

Danny was stunned into silence. Everyone else in the band had to read sheet music or tab for the chords, and even then they made a lot of mistakes. Even sticking to a basic rhythm was a challenge for the fledging group. Danny became concerned that he and the other band members wouldn't be good enough for Retina Boy. Maybe they should practice before Retina Boy joined so they wouldn't sound so amateurish.

Danny couldn't wrap his head around the fact that this blind kid could be so talented. He himself struggled at times with the drums—sometimes while playing he'd miss a cymbal or a tom—yet he wasn't even completely blind. He had lost significant peripheral vision and couldn't see well at night. Inevitably, the constriction of his vision would continue. He knew by the time he was forty he'd likely need a cane or a guide dog. None of the doctors told him that; it's what all the retinitis pigmentosa articles on the foundation's website said. But then again, if the gene therapy worked, his vision would be saved.

Most baffling for Danny was Retina Boy's ability to navigate without a cane or dog. He'd never seen such a thing, and no one at the conference who was completely blind could get around without any help. It didn't make sense to Danny that this kid could. Was the kid lying? Maybe he did have a little vision and was just faking it. And those crazy blue-green eyes. What were those all about?

Retina Boy was also apprehensive about Danny—not that he found anything wrong with his new pal. It was that he never really had a friend other than Marcy, and now he'd be getting together with Danny and these other guys to play music. Would they take the blind kid in? Many boys his age could be so cliquish. Some were pranksters. Others were just mean. He imagined them hiding his guitar or calling him 'googly eyes.' Hopefully, everyone would get along.

Chapter 11

For all intents and purposes, Zooba operated under an oligarchy, a group of a few dozen political leaders who had their hooks in everything. For fifty generations, the planet had been governed by a democracy with citizen-elected officials, but that system suffered from widespread corruption and gridlock. However, thanks to the collapse of democracy, there were no longer any courts, judges, or attorneys—just the Zog, which was essentially the government, police, legal authority, and public-service system all rolled into one. Zoobans tolerated the authoritarian regime that ruled the planet. As long as the citizens were able to indulge in hyperconsumption, they were content.

A vast majority of Zoobans were law-abiding because they had no idea what the unpredictable Zog would do if they were caught committing a crime. Often, the sentence for serious crimes—murders, violent assaults, and rapes—was death by lethal injection. And the authorities didn't dilly-dally; a Zooban could go from being a suspect to being put to death in a matter of a few weeks.

For other crimes—most of which had some financial or economic component—the punishments varied widely. Some big-time corporate embezzlers got a slap on the wrist; others were incarcerated indefinitely. The same was true for small-time crooks. While the penalties were usually minimal for stealing and shoplifting, if the authorities felt someone was a persistent nuisance or could be a threat for a more serious crime, they might serve some major time.

With so much time on his hands, and virtually no income, shoplifting became an avocation for Doug. He had a weakness for electronic gizmos, especially radios and audio players, and every few months new and improved models came on the market. Zooban telecommunication experts were steadily getting better at picking up radio, television, and internet signals from Earth, and there were always new devices developed that could take more of the planet's digital content and convert it to audio for the Zooban population.

Doug had been caught once for stealing a pack of tiny disposable speakers that were placed inside the ears. It wasn't an exorbitantly expensive product, and the Zog decided they didn't want to make a big ruckus about the Earthling being a shoplifter. So they let him go. They felt they had nothing to gain by drawing attention to him. Why make an Earthling look bad? If humans appeared difficult, it might dissuade Zoobans from wanting to invade their planet.

After the bust, Doug learned that the shoplifting detection controllers were small red panels at the front of each store. Zellie heard from a friend that the system detected when merchandise left the store without being paid for, and it captured a unique electromagnetic image of the shoplifter, which could be converted into audio data for identification by Zog detectives. Proprietors primarily entered only valuable items into the system, so it was relatively easy to lift food, clothing, or personal products.

Doug found a store near his apartment without a red panel in front and began frequenting it for shoplifting excursions. He usually lifted just one item at a time that wasn't expensive and likely not monitored by the security system. However, his false sense of confidence led him to go after an item of value, a new radio, which was in fact secured. That store's detection controller happened to be in a storage room in the back, out of his view.

The radio, known as the NFL-3790, was about two by three inches, ultrathin, and programmed to receive and archive every National Football

League game over the last five seasons. There were similar devices for various baseball, soccer, basketball, and hockey leagues. Most Zooban fans followed a single sport, maybe two, so many radios and receivers were programmed to capture only one sport or league. With a pittance for an allowance, Doug wouldn't be able to afford the NFL-3790 for several months. And there'd likely be a new and improved version of the device on the market by the time he had enough currency to pay for the NFL-3790.

Unfortunately, Doug's shoplifting luck ran out. He knew it when two Zohag officers—tall, bulky males with long dark hair and thick beards, clad in their familiarly official gray robes—towered next to him as he stood in his doorway, having answered his apartment's entry alert buzzer. The brutes looked almost like twins, though Zeglo had a larger, rounder belly. He tightly gripped a disabling wand by his side, pointing it down to the ground. Ziglo had discouraged his partner from using any force but agreed that it was good to be ready, just in case. It would look bad to their superiors if they would somehow let the Earthling get away, even if only temporarily.

Doug had become worried when his apartment entry buzzer went off. No one ever came to visit other than Zellie, and his voice recognition security system was programmed to let her enter on her own. At first, Doug was relieved the unexpected guests weren't scientists coming to extract his other eye.

Ziglo and Zeglo, both of whom cosupervised several crime units in the local district, told Doug only that he was being incarcerated for theft and legal authorities would more thoroughly interrogate him later on.

This was uncharted territory for Doug. He'd never talked to anyone who'd been arrested by the Zog, nor did he have any counsel to advise him about what to say and what not to say.

This was also an unusual case for Ziglo and Zeglo. Never before had they processed a non-Zooban. As a result, they were instructed to file a preliminary report of their findings to higher Zog command, who would make the ultimate decision about how to punish the human shoplifter.

"Your name is Doug, and you are an Earthling living in District 497623, Building 84, Unit ZA7—correct?" asked Ziglo, as he stood with Zeglo in a small holding area of the Zohag, dimly lit by ambient light coming in through a ventilation panel on the outside wall.

"Uh, yeah," replied Doug, who sat on a short stool in front of the two officials.

"According to Zolobob, the owner of Store X37 in the same district, the security system identified you as the shoplifter of an NFL-3790—correct?" asked Ziglo.

"Zolobob? What kind of crazy name is that?" interjected Zeglo before Doug could answer. "He must be from District 497640. They're so bizarre over there! You know they listen to tennis matches?"

"Will you please shut up? I'm trying to process the criminal," Ziglo said, aggravated. "Anyway, Zolobob is a female and her voice is actually very... uh... pleasant."

"Oh, sorry Zig. But if you end up touching her, and she's nice, let me know if she has any sisters."

"I'll be sure to report back on my progress with Zolobob. Now, Zeglo, may I please proceed with the Earthling, here?"

"Of course," answered Zeglo.

"Now, Doug, is it true that you removed an NFL-3790 from Store X37 without paying for it?"

"Yeah, I guess so," Doug answered. "I don't remember the exact model number, but it's the new NFL radio."

"OK, that's good enough. That is a clear admission. Do you have anything to say about this charge?"

Doug looked down in thought for a few seconds. He had no idea how to respond.

Zeglo cleared this throat. "How about saying, 'Go Browns,' and then we can get out of here and go to lunch?"

"When did you start getting into the NFL?" Ziglo asked Zeglo in surprise.

"Oh, since the spouse started listening to it. She likes those announcers—Michaels and Madden. Who knew?"

"Huh, who knew?" said Ziglo. "Well, anyway, it's into the holding cell for you, Doug. And we'll be getting back to you with a report from headquarters."

After a long period of deliberation, the authorities sentenced Doug to solitary incarceration in the Zohag. Even though the young Earthling had been cooperative, they became worried that his bad behavior would only get worse. They didn't want him out in public drawing attention if he committed further crimes or misdeeds, especially if they were more serious. Nor did they want him interacting with other prisoners who might harm him or whom he might hurt. They didn't know how Zooban inmates would react to having an Earthling in their midst.

To minimize the emotional strain on him, they agreed to his request to let Zellie visit for an hour every few days. They allowed her to bring him small gifts, usually food. She managed to smuggle in small vials of zing in zoofeejee. A vial held enough for about three hits, so he indulged in one hit every evening. The zing and her visits were just enough to keep him from losing his sanity. The authorities allowed him to have a few radios, including the very NFL-3790 that led to his incarceration. However, in a cruel and ironic twist of fate, the device stopped working the day the new football season was to be uploaded.

While Ziglo was now a veteran criminal processor, and well respected by his peers and leaders for being an effective retriever, he began to have second thoughts about his job and the legitimacy and fairness of the law-enforcement system. Yes, the number of bad-intentioned, law-breaking citizens was steadily increasing in his district and across the planet. But with those arrests, the number of innocent Zoobans getting locked up—for example, those who happened to be near the scene of a theft or burglary and happened to be misidentified as the perpetrator—was on the upswing. When guilt was uncertain for a given suspect, more often than not, the order from above was "to put them away—get them out of the community."

Zoobans, in general, were becoming more uneasy about the state of the planet. While most didn't publicly question or criticize their leaders' long-term strategy of an Earth invasion to save Zooba, a growing minority of citizens began to doubt the feasibility of it. Not only did they find the invasion itself morally reprehensible, but they also couldn't imagine how Earth would avoid being devastated by the invasion despite claims by leadership that major destruction was preventable. Would Earthlings really give up without much of a fight and their own violent response? They were not hesitant to use force as a means of influence and control.

In the meantime, Zooba's pollution continued to worsen. Rates of pulmonary and skin disease were on the rise, with citizens reluctant to take the precautions—such as wearing masks, avoiding the outdoors, and washing and scrubbing with potent cleansers three times a day—to minimize risk.

Though he never told anyone, Ziglo was troubled by Doug's incarceration. The poor Earthling had been kidnapped, disfigured, and locked up indefinitely, all because of the Zog's dysfunction and paranoia. But what could he do? It made no sense to file an appeal on Doug's behalf—that would be political suicide. And he had no one to confide in to get his feelings off his chest. Zeglo was affable, but intellectually little more than a bag of rocks and not likely to empathize with his discontent.

Ziglo decided the best he could do was take care of himself and try to find some enjoyment is his mundane life as a Zooban bachelor. Maybe he'd stop by Zolobob's store and make sure she hadn't had any more shoplifters. Maybe he'd ask her out if she seemed friendly and amenable. It would be so nice to reach out and touch a new female.

Chapter 12

The band's first order of business—determining its name—had largely been settled before all its members ever met. Marcy heard Dr. Strong's keynote address in Chicago in which he described Danny's genetic retinal disease. She was captivated by the name of Danny's mutated gene and the light-absorbing protein it expressed: rhodopsin. What name could be cooler for a band with two members with retinal diseases? Doing research online, she learned that rhodopsin was known as "visual purple" because of its color, and it enabled people to see in the dark.

"I think it's the perfect name for you guys because it's in the retina and helps you see and you could also make purple your official color!" she wrote in an email to Retina Boy and Danny. "It comes from the Greek words for visual and purple. Pretty cool, huh?"

Danny and Retina Boy were immediately on board with the idea, and the other members agreed to it at their first practice in Danny's basement, before they played their first note together.

"Like, I don't totally understand what it means, but it sounds fine to me," said Justin, the band's keyboard player and best-trained member. He'd been taking piano lessons since the age of six, and like Retina Boy he could pick up a tune by ear and quickly memorize it. A boyish and shy soul, Justin was more into the Beatles and Elton John than edgier groups like Led Zeppelin and Black Sabbath but was usually content playing just about anything. Not much for conversation, especially in large groups, Justin preferred connecting with people through his keyboards.

"Yeah, I think it sounds pretty cool," said Jake, nodding in agreement. The bass player was popular with girls, even those a class or two ahead of him, thanks to his rugged jawline and patch of hair on his chin. "I was thinking we could call ourselves 'Slush Magnet,' but I dunno, your idea works. What is it, again?"

"Rhodopsin," said Danny rolling his eyes.

The rambunctious Sammy, still feeling the sting of losing his role as lead guitarist, relegated to vocals only, said, "Yeah, whatever. No one else will ever pick that name, that's for sure." Neither he nor Jake had much natural talent or discipline—they just liked the cachet of being in a band. Though they would never admit it, they were hoping that Retina Boy's arrival would help them sound more like a real band and elevate their status at school, and ultimately attract more girls.

While choosing a name came easy, playing decent music proved quite challenging at first. Rhodopsin sounded like the amateurish unpracticed group of fourteen- and fifteen-year-olds that it was. During its first practice, it took them more than an hour to get through "Smoke on the Water" without completely falling apart. Danny had chosen the song because it was easy, and perhaps it could be Rhodopsin's signature song because it was from the band Deep Purple.

Retina Boy saw quickly that the band had two big problems. They sounded clunky and brash because, in part, of the basement's low ceiling and tiled floor. They also had difficulty keeping time and playing together, an issue that Danny acknowledged had always plagued them. Though Danny played at a reasonable tempo, the other members, except for Retina Boy, had a tough time keeping up with him.

Also, Retina Boy's talent and ease put him in another universe altogether and only exacerbated their lack of confidence and continuity. His effortless playing was downright intimidating to the other members.

"This kid must be cloned from Jimmy Page," Sammy quipped halfway through the band's first practice. "Or maybe he's from another planet."

"No, but my uncle is Ritchie Blackmore," said Retina Boy, trying unsuccessfully to get a laugh.

Realizing he needed to take a different tack to gain respect, Retina Boy put down his Stratocaster for the rest of the practice. Rather than dazzle his new friends with his amazing chops, he'd help them get in synch. They all knew they desperately needed help and that Retina Boy was the one to give it. It was obvious to everyone, including Retina Boy, that he should become the band's leader.

For the next half hour, he had all the members slow down their tempo so it wouldn't be so difficult for them to stay together and, hopefully, they'd make fewer mistakes. The good news was that not only was Danny a solid drummer, but he was also flexible and patient, willing to follow Retina Boy's instructions. In turn, the other members followed Danny's rhythmic lead. Retina Boy hadn't pulled this strategy out of thin air; he was simply following the same approach Will used with him: play the tune slowly until you eliminate the mistakes, then you can pick up the tempo.

It took three more hour-long practices once a week until Rhodopsin got "Smoke on the Water" down reasonably well. However, the milestone gave them confidence and enthusiasm. They learned that through practice and Retina Boy's guidance, they could sound like something that resembled a rock band.

"I think we should do 'Purple Haze' next," suggested Sammy after the band members agreed that they'd hit the mark with "Smoke on the Water." "I mean, it's got purple in the title, and it's Hendrix—you know, it's a cool song."

"Yeah, that's a cool idea," said Retina Boy. "But we also need to keep practicing 'Smoke' for a while. We're doing it pretty well, but we can do better. Let's really know it by heart. Yuh know?"

Everyone nodded in agreement.

"And maybe we can practice twice a week—maybe Tuesday and Thursday," Retina Boy added. "That's if your parents are OK with us using the basement so much, Danny."

"Sure, they'll be cool with it."

Everyone else nodded reluctantly. Retina Boy sensed that his buddies were not thrilled with the idea of more work, but if no one was going to say anything in opposition, he'd just move forward with the plan. Hopefully, they'd show up when he asked them to.

Retina Boy never expected his leadership role to come so naturally. Before forming the band, listening and playing music had just been a personal avocation. Except for school, he didn't have many opportunities to interact socially with groups of kids. However, because of his talent, knowledge, and humility—he never judged his band members for their abilities or limitations—he had gained respect.

Also, without purposely using it to his advantage, at least at first, Retina Boy found that people, including his bandmates, were sometimes reluctant to challenge him because he was blind. They were concerned that he didn't understand situations as well because he couldn't see facial expressions and body language. Even though they meant no harm, they felt sorry for him because of his blindness. But with zill, even his limited grasp of it, he could sense the mood and emotions of a person or small gathering surprisingly well.

Over time, Marcy, the band members, and other close acquaintances picked up on the fact that Retina Boy wasn't as "in the dark" as they had initially thought. But awareness of his unique "sensibility" just elicited more respect.

And then there were his otherworldly aquamarine eyes. No one could help but be fascinated by them. Even Marcy, who'd known him for years, would occasionally stare into his hypnotic eyes in wonder. Yes, he had an affliction that made him blind, but she was certain there was something else going on that made him special. She just couldn't quite put her finger on it.

Chapter 13

The contest was called the *Des Moines Halloween Battle of the Bands*, and though Will had never heard Rhodopsin play, he knew they likely wouldn't win—most of the other contestants were in high school and in more established groups—but nor would they embarrass themselves with Retina Boy on lead guitar. He was as good as any of the older kids, perhaps better.

"I think going in front of a live audience would be a good step up for Rhodopsin," he said to Retina Boy at the end of a lesson. "I'm not a judge this year, but in the past there were always a couple of bands that really sucked and a couple that were reasonably good. My guess is that you'll fall somewhere in between. But I think playing in front of a live audience will help get you to the next level."

Rhodopsin had been playing for less than two months and had two songs solidly under their belt. They needed three songs for the contest. One recording for the first round, one tune performed live for the semis on Saturday, and one for the finals on Sunday. They had less than three weeks until the deadline, so whatever they chose to learn had to be relatively simple.

When Retina Boy arrived at the next practice, Danny informed him that Sammy and Jake had just called to say that they wouldn't be available that afternoon. They had after-school detention for passing notes back and forth. "What's crazy is that they sit like five rows apart!" said Danny as the three remaining band members sat in his basement wondering how to proceed.

Retina Boy folded his arms and shook his head. "Shit," he muttered. Danny and Justin had never seen their usually cool-headed friend so miffed.

As he often did between takes to burn off nervous energy, Justin tinkered with scales and short phrases from various songs at his keyboards. As he broke into the intro to "Let It Be"—the iconic chord sequence of C, G, Am, and F—a large gray tabby with one eye sauntered into the large basement room heading straight for Retina Boy, who was sitting on a wooden folding chair.

"Oh, that's Mongo," said Danny as the cat rubbed up against Retina Boy's leg. "Yeah, my parents picked him up from the shelter about a month ago. He usually doesn't come down here. He's got feline leukemia, so he probably won't live very long. But he's pretty cool."

"Maybe he likes Paul McCartney," said Justin. He smiled and continued to play and sing softly, as if crooning for the cat. "Let it be, let it be, let it be, yeah let it be. Speaking words of wisdom to Mongo, let it be." He sang sincerely and effortlessly with a melancholic undertone.

It was the first time Retina Boy really took notice of Justin performing solo—especially his smooth, soulful vocals—given he'd only played keyboard in background roles in Rhodopsin's first two songs. Retina Boy hadn't considered a ballad for the band's third song for the contest—the other members had been lobbying to do a Zeppelin song next—but Justin's voice was like a newly discovered secret weapon. Not only would "Let It Be" be easy for everyone to learn, the band didn't even need Sammy or Jake to begin practicing that afternoon.

During the next practice two days later, as Rhodopsin began its third take of "Let It Be," Danny's parents for the first time came down the stairs to listen to their son and his friends. The song was more their speed than Rhodopsin's harder numbers, and the boys covered it with confidence and ease.

Even Mongo showed up to enjoy what were becoming regular affectionate encounters with Retina Boy's leg, especially when the band played ballads. When Retina Boy wasn't holding his guitar, the cat would jump up on his lap and purr loudly as he rubbed its head. Animals could be problematic for Retina Boy, especially unleashed dogs, which often ran up to him and barked incessantly, sensing that he wasn't quite like other humans. But Mongo made friends with him.

None of Rhodopsin's first fans—parental and feline—were exactly music geeks, but "Let It Be" touched them as it did the two hundred kids and parents who attended the contest finals at the Drake University auditorium.

The young teenage boys in Rhodopsin weren't as showy or pretentious as most of their high school competitors, who sported hats, sunglasses, dark makeup, and other distracting effects. Rhodopsin's skinny lads just wore T-shirts, jeans, and sneakers, and played with concentration one might expect from serious musicians. They weren't animated on the stage. Retina Boy's disciplined persona had rubbed off on the other members of the band; without realizing it, they, too, were focused on the music and their instruments rather than how they were perceived by friends and classmates.

Not only was the audience moved by Justin's poignant keyboards and vocals during "Let It Be," Retina Boy, like a cleanup hitter, brought everyone home with his charged, anthemic guitar solo before the song's final verse. The crowd was transfixed by his hypnotic eyes and the speed and agility with which he moved his fingers up and down the neck of the instrument as he cranked out long, roaring notes. He looked like a stoic, seasoned pro who had been doing gigs for years. No one, not even his parents, knew he'd been practicing that thirty second solo over and over every night during the past week up in his bedroom with no amp.

Rhodopsin's strong performance earned them second place. They were beat out by a group of high school seniors who played Zeppelin's "Heartbreaker" and "Going to California" for the semi and final rounds.

"You guys were brilliant. Honestly, I thought it was a toss-up," said Will as the boys packed up their instruments. "And I have to say, picking a Beatles classic for your final song was a great move."

"I can't believe it. We've been playing for barely three months!" said Retina Boy smiling broadly, already thinking about what song Rhodopsin should learn next.

"Well, you guys stayed within yourselves. You didn't try to do too much. I think that was really important," Will replied, patting Justin's shoulder. "But it's obvious you guys practiced a lot. You were really tight. Discipline is the key. Most of the great bands had it, including those talented boys from Liverpool. They played thousands of gigs before they made it big."

Chapter 14

Zellie sang along to the bouncy, gleeful vocals of George Michael—
"Wake me up before you go-go, don't keep me hanging on like a yo-yo"—as
she carefully slid a vial of zing into the gooey center of a zoofeejee. The
trick she learned more than a year ago was to put the tiny vial through the
seam in the crust on the ends of the pastry. Luckily, no guard at the Zohag
had ever examined the zoofeejee, though they did occasionally comment on
the smell, trying to guess which bakery vendor she had bought them from.
Because Doug was apart from the other prisoners, Zellie entered the facility through an infrequently used auxiliary side door, which typically had the
same two guards at the security station. After a few weeks of her visits, they
got to know Zellie and only asked to examine her bag using a baton that
only detected explosives and weapons.

As she wrapped the zoofeejee up for delivery to Doug, the broadcast
from the 1980s music channel was interrupted for a special news report:
"This is a breaking news bulletin from the Zog Information Bureau.
Scientists have moved closer to enabling Zoobans to see with their eyes.
Genetic researchers recently discovered variants in four gene pairs that
are responsible for the development of retinas in Earthlings. Researchers
believe that by correcting or modifying just one copy of each gene pair, they
may someday give us eyesight by empowering us to grow retinas. They also
identified a small number of other genetic differences between humans and

Zoobans, but only four appear to be related to retinal development. More details will be forthcoming as we receive them."

The news took Zellie's breath away. Like many Zoobans, she'd been waiting to hear updates on the plans to invade Earth. But this report on the genetics behind retinas was completely unexpected—she had no idea what to make of it. What would it be like to see with her eyes? What would Doug look like? What would Zooba look like? But she struggled to imagine how this development might change Doug's fate for the better. If anything, the scientists might want to do even more experiments on him. Perhaps they would take his other eye.

In the coming days, Zooba became abuzz with excitement and conjecture. Many Zoobans believed that vision would better equip them to invade Earth. It would even the playing field with Earthlings. Many Zoobans believed that planning for the takeover should be accelerated.

The discovery of the four genetic variations also led to confusion and ambivalence within the highest echelon of the Zog. Not all the leaders understood right away that a gene therapy to correct the variations might only be successful, if at all, in utero or in vitro just a few days after conception. These four genes—which did not express as much protein in Zoobans as they did in humans—needed to be modified or replaced at the earliest stages of retinal development if Zoobans were ever to see. In other words, there would be no treatment for the existing population. Some leaders feared that if scientists decided to administer gene therapy to newly conceived Zoobans, the youth would have the advantage of vision over the elders for several decades, potentially threatening their power.

The Zog's top brass eventually decided to limit information about how and when a genetic treatment might be implemented. Their spin was "more research is needed to make a vision-enabling therapy available to the general public."

When Zellie arrived at the Zohag to visit Doug, the guards quickly scanned her large satchel with the baton as they always did, but then they asked her to wait and take a seat before going in. The lead officer said something quietly into the radio on his wrist. Zellie became anxious; she'd gone through this entry process dozens of times previously but was never held back. She was convinced that news of the genetic breakthrough had put Doug in danger. It made sense that they'd want to perform more experiments on him before trying out a new therapy on Zoobans. She sat quietly, feeling afraid and helpless. She did her best not to appear suspiciously nervous.

After about ten minutes, a high-pitched "she can go in" came from the lead officer's wrist radio. The loudness of the unanticipated message caused him to flinch in surprise. Zellie and the other officer smiled. "You heard. It's OK to go visit your Earthling buddy," the lead said. "There's another visitor with him—that's why you had to wait. We didn't know if he could have two visitors at one time."

As a guard unlocked and retracted the sliding door to Doug's room, a large male sitting in a chair next to Doug stood up.

"Hello, my name's Ziglo," he said.

The guard left the room and closed the door, locking everyone in.

"I'm just visiting," Ziglo explained. "You must be Zellie. Doug's told me a lot about you."

"Yeah. He used to be with the Zog, if you can believe that," Doug snapped, sitting on the edge of his bed.

"Yes, that's true," Ziglo interjected. "But I left a short time ago—on my own terms. Honestly, I was getting depressed with the job, though I didn't tell my managers that."

"So you're visiting Doug? But why?" Zellie took a chair and put down her bag.

"Yeah. I know this all seems weird, but I was in criminal retrieval and processing. I actually processed Doug," Ziglo explained. "Really, I felt bad about it. Doug doesn't deserve to be locked up like this. I don't think he's a danger to anyone."

Zellie scooted in her chair closer to Doug and Ziglo. Whispering, she said, "Aren't you worried that they're listening in on us? Uh, maybe you should be more careful about what you say?"

"I doubt it. This isn't a normal incarceration cell. There's no monitoring system. At least there wasn't when I was still with the Zog. They were running out of room for prisoners, so they stuck him in here. Used to be a recreational room. It's very low security."

The serendipitously combined visit from Ziglo and Zellie was the most social activity Doug had had in years. No one but Zellie ever visited him at the facility. To have two visitors at the same time was exhilarating for him but overwhelming at the same time. Doug tugged on his long, tangled hair and scraggily beard as he sat on his bed.

Doug was nearly seventeen years old and had grown heavier from lack of exercise and poor diet. To other humans, he would have looked like a caveman who got caught in a time warp and plopped down in the twenty-first century. He looked Zooban.

"So, Doug, there's something you should know, though I'm not sure what it will really mean. Maybe Ziglo already told you," Zellie said, turning toward Ziglo, then to Doug. "The Zooban researchers found the genes that give normal retinas to you and all other humans."

"Wow! That's unbelievable!" Doug exclaimed, springing up to his feet in surprise. "So do you think they can enable Zoobans to see? Maybe someday?"

"I guess," answered Ziglo. "Everyone's pretty pumped up about the news. However, there are no details on how Zoobans might actually get the genes. I don't know if everyone would get them, or maybe just the children of the wealthy. I think there is a lot they haven't figured out."

"I just hope they leave me alone. I don't want to be part of any more experiments," Doug said, realizing the breakthrough might mean more experiments on him. He sat back down. He was worried that the scientists might take his other eye, but he wouldn't even suggest the possibility for fear it would somehow have a better chance of becoming a reality.

Neither Zellie nor Ziglo were comfortable responding to Doug's comment. They knew that the powers that be had little concern for his well-being. Anything could happen to him.

Zellie changed the subject. "So, Ziglo, what are you doing now that you've left the Zog?" she asked.

Ziglo grinned bashfully. "Well, it's kind of crazy, but I'm working for a vendor, helping her with inventory, cleaning, and other odd jobs. Actually, it's the same place where Doug stole the radio from."

"No shit," said Doug. "How did that happen?"

"Well, after you were incarcerated, I went back to ask the owner out. Her name is Zolobob."

Zellie laughed out loud. "Zolobob? That's her name? You're kidding me?"

"Look, she's originally from another sector, but she's really nice," Ziglo replied in Zolobob's defense. "And hanging out with her sure beats putting away criminals... and innocent citizens like Doug."

Zellie cleared her throat. "Sorry, I wasn't trying to be mean."

"I know. It's OK." Ziglo stood up. "Well, I need to head on out, or I'll be late meeting Zolobob for lunch."

"Yeah, I also have to get going. I have three orphans on my schedule today. I'm a caretaker. That's how I met Doug. I was assigned his case. Now I just visit him here."

"Well, now you have another visitor, Doug. Me. I'm going to try and stop by at least once a week and see how you're doing. Is there anything I can bring you?"

"Sure. I'd really like another NFL radio. But I know they're not cheap."

"I think I can get one from Zolobob without the profit markup. She'd want you to have it. She had no idea that the punishment for your shoplifting would be so harsh. She feels bad about what happened to you."

Doug smiled in appreciation. He felt great to have a new friend—another Zooban who actually cared about him.

Ziglo knocked on the door, prompting the guard to let him and Zellie leave. As Zellie walked out behind Ziglo, Doug noticed for the first time how her hips moved when she walked. Having put on a little weight herself recently, her pants were tighter and revealed more of her curvy figure. Doug had always found her attractive, more so than most Zooban females. But this was a new, powerful feeling, an arousal. He had a desire to be next to her, to touch her well-rounded bottom.

Even from twenty feet away Zellie could sense Doug's desire. She turned her head around to face him. Her eyes, normally aquamarine, had turned deep indigo. Zellie grinned seductively as she passed through the doorway of the cell.

Chapter 15

To no one's surprise, Marcy aced the SATs. She also earned an A in every class through the middle of her junior year, except one: racquetball. She signed up for the class just to see how the administration would handle racquetball for a student in a wheelchair. It was her snarky way of drawing attention to kids with disabilities. She was certain they wouldn't accommodate her and would force her to enroll in something like swimming, which she'd taken twice before and which, she'd never admit, she had actually enjoyed.

To her surprise, Mr. Gajewski, a.k.a. Mr. G, the phys ed instructor, accepted her enrollment into racquetball and had every intention of making the class work for her. His first challenge was getting her wheelchair onto the court—it didn't fit through the door. So he had two students carry her in while he collapsed the chair and brought it through the doorway. After the other kids were paired off for matches, he tried to volley with Marcy, hitting the ball softly to her forehand. Though she didn't have to move her chair to reach his shots—Mr. G was very pleased with his accuracy and light touch—she struggled to connect with the ball. During the second class, Marcy muttered expletives when she missed and at one point yelled, "This is a fucking exercise in futility, Mr. G!" So he took Marcy off the court and had her take attendance and tabulate match scores for the remainder of the semester.

To Marcy's dismay, he gave her a B for the class. Though she appealed the grade, Mr. G noted that he had been generous in not disciplining her for cursing. "If I went by the book, I would have suspended Marcy," he wrote to the principal in his rebuttal. "I completely understand that Marcy is a top student and has physical limitations. However, a student who uses inappropriate language does not deserve an "A." She certainly should understand that. I don't tolerate it from any other students."

Despite the distraction of her imperfect grade point average, next year's likely valedictorian had her sights set on the country's best undergraduate astronomy programs, namely MIT, Berkeley, Harvard, and Stanford. She hadn't ruled out the University of Oxford, but the UK seemed far away from home to her. Perhaps she'd consider going overseas for her doctorate.

Retina Boy and the other members of Rhodopsin were planning to stay in Iowa for college. Their hope was that they could continue practicing and doing gigs at dances and parties during the summer and holiday breaks. Perhaps when all the members turned eighteen, in another year or so, they could start playing clubs and larger venues. But they knew if they had any hopes of making it big, they'd need to start writing their own music. Although they practiced regularly and had developed a repertoire of a few dozen songs, no one had taken the leap yet of composing original material.

Retina Boy hadn't been thinking about how he and Marcy would be apart for much of the time after the end of next summer. Eighteen months seemed far into the future, and he was distracted by schoolwork and Rhodopsin practices. Though Marcy couldn't wait to go off to college and take on bigger academic challenges, she steadily grew insecure about her future with Retina Boy and worried about what might happen when they were apart.

The day before Valentine's Day was unseasonably warm in Des Moines. The high reached sixty-two degrees. Retina Boy and Marcy decided to get out in the beautiful, sunny weather and go for a late-afternoon excursion next to the park. As they were walking, a strong, warm breeze came from the southeast and blew across the empty fields. Dark clouds began forming in the northwest sky. Rain was forecasted to start at about eight o'clock that evening and turn to snow at around eleven. The weather pundits predicted four to six inches of snow by sunrise.

"These are my favorite days. You know, in winter, when all the snow melts. It feels so warm," said Marcy as they slowly made their way up the desolate path, occasionally sloshing through puddles that Retina Boy could not see. "It's surreal. Out here it's like we're on another planet."

"Uh-huh," answered Retina Boy, who was thinking about Danny's gene-therapy surgery next week. Hopefully, the treatment would work and save his friend's vision. Hopefully, Danny wouldn't be out of commission for too long. The band would have a difficult time practicing without its drummer.

"You know, we should do something special for Valentine's Day. Maybe go out to dinner," Marcy suggested. "It's Saturday, so maybe my parents can take us somewhere. Maybe some place really nice. They don't have to stay with us. Just drop us off."

"Uh-huh," Retina Boy said again, still distracted by his thoughts about Danny.

Marcy became annoyed by his lack of attention to her. "Are you even listening to me?"

"Oh, sorry, Marcy," he answered matter-of-factly. "Yeah, dinner. That would be cool."

While she and Retina Boy were inseparable, they'd never had much of a physical romance. The strength of their relationship was in their friend-ship. Marcy had thought about sex on occasion, especially over the last year, but she was self-conscious about her chair and immobility and was afraid to initiate anything more than a kiss. She feared that if she did make the first move and Retina Boy wasn't interested, it might scare him off and jeopardize their friendship. The idea of going to dinner for Valentine's Day was by no means a sexual advance, but Marcy thought of it as a romantic suggestion, something in that direction. It took some courage for her to suggest it.

As a Zooban, Retina Boy sometimes sensed Marcy's physical interests, but he would sexually bloom a little later than humans, so he hadn't been interested in pursuing anything romantic with her. The light simply hadn't come on for him yet.

At the moment, however, he knew Marcy was unusually angry and hurt—his casual apology had only made matters worse. She began tearing up. He stopped pushing the chair and walked around it to face her.

"Look, Marcy, I'm really sorry. Dinner would be really cool," he said. He crouched down and put his hand on her knee. "C'mon, don't cry. We'll have an awesome Valentine's Day. I promise."

Marcy thought of a million things to say, including "I love you," but was too upset to get anything out. She feared more than ever that she might lose Retina Boy, that he didn't love her, that he was getting bored, and that he'd leave her. She continued to cry as she put her hand on his cheek and gazed into his aquamarine eyes.

With her touch, Retina Boy felt a surge of warmth and excitement throughout his body. But he had difficulty reconciling his arousal with her sadness. He felt guilty about feeling so good.

Marcy had no idea what was happening for Retina Boy at the moment, but when his eyes suddenly turned to a deep purple blue, she gasped in surprise and fell over unconscious in her chair.

Chapter 16

Danny's parents, Meg and Marc Pullman, sat directly across from Marcy and Retina Boy in the expansive hospital waiting area for nearly three hours before Dr. Strong came out through the double doors of the ophthalmology surgery center dressed in green scrubs, holding an electronic tablet.

"Well, the procedure went very well," he said as he tapped the screen of the device a few times before looking up at the Pullmans. "We injected the vector containing healthy copies of rhodopsin underneath Danny's retina without any complications. As I explained, the bleb, the injected liquid, creates a retinal detachment, but that should be temporary. We just need Danny to stay on his back for a while until the vector gets absorbed into the retina."

Meg cleared her throat. "So how's his vision? When do you think it will return to the way it was before the surgery?" she said.

"Should be back to baseline in a few days," said Dr. Strong. "Like I said, the procedure went well. The detachment should resolve without any problem."

"But it will be a year or two until you know if the therapy is working, right?" asked Marc Pullman, sitting up in his chair.

"Yeah, Mr. Pullman, that's our best guess at the moment," said Dr. Strong, nodding his head. "Again, our hope is that we stabilize vision in the treated eye. Maybe we'll see some restoration of vision, if we're lucky, but the idea is to halt disease progression. Bottom line is we'll follow changes in vision and retinal structure in the treated eye versus the fellow eye. If the treatment appears to be working, we'll inject the fellow eye."

"Well, we're really grateful that you got him into the trial," said Meg. "His vision has really gone downhill over the last year. He's been willing to try just about anything."

"You have to keep in mind that this is a clinical trial. We're still learning about the therapy," explained Dr. Strong. "With that said, we're hopeful it will work."

Dr. Strong noticed that Marc Pullman had become distracted by something on the other side of the waiting room. He looked astonished. The doctor turned around to see what had captured Marc's attention. At first, Dr. Strong didn't notice anything remarkable, but then he saw that Retina Boy's eyes had turned to indigo. Marcy was sitting next to him with her eyes closed and her hand resting on the middle of his thigh.

As a retinal expert, Dr. Strong wasn't familiar with all the conditions of the iris. He did know that eyes normally didn't change color, and the suggestion that they did was a myth. They may *look* like they have changed color due to unusual lighting or a person's clothes, but Retina Boy was wearing a gray-and-black-checkered flannel shirt. And the waiting room lighting was soft and natural.

Dr. Strong stared at Retina Boy for a few seconds, perplexed by what he'd never seen before—indigo eyes. He'd never heard of anyone with that eye color. Given that he had to prep for another surgery, he didn't have time to investigate the situation further. Perhaps he'd talk to some of his colleagues who did anterior segment research, though they might think he was crazy. Many other ophthalmologists had taken notice of Retina Boy's unique aquamarine eyes and knew about his unusual retinas. They knew this kid was different. Regardless, he'd be seeing Retina Boy in a few weeks, so he could do a thorough exam then. Maybe he'd order some blood work just to make sure there wasn't something serious going on. It would be interesting to see what his eyes looked like when he came back for his appointment. Would they have reverted back to aquamarine?

Dr. Strong turned back around to face the Pullmans and said, "I'll have a nurse come out in a few minutes to let you go back to see Danny. Sorry, gotta run." Then he hurried off, back through the double doors.

But Marcy already knew what Dr. Strong would never know: Retina Boy's eyes changed color when he became sexually aroused—and in recent weeks, it hadn't taken much excitement to make it happen. The phenomenon had been shocking initially and had caused her to faint in the park. She saw it happen again a couple of days later when they were making out in his basement. It happened a third time later that week when he gave her a long good night kiss on her porch.

After Marcy had told him what was happening to his eyes, Retina Boy became self-conscious.

"Everybody's gonna know when I'm horny!" he had said.

But Marcy convinced him that only she'd know, and she wouldn't tell anyone about what she called his "superpower." "You just better behave yourself when we're around other girls," she warned him. "I'll know what you're thinking."

"Don't worry," Retina Boy replied reassuringly. "I'll only be thinking about you."

Chapter 17

The Zog's fears about the potential impact of the retinal-gene discovery on its citizenry were beginning to come true. Zoobans wanted to see, and they wanted to see as soon as possible. They had become frustrated by the lack of information about the development of a vision-enabling therapy and how and when they and their loved ones would get it. They began to organize small protests in the commercial sectors to discourage consumption; they knew economic boycotts would capture the Zog's attention. However, most surprising and alarming to the Zog was that interest in the Earth invasion also began to wane because of what they called "the vision distraction." Zoobans were becoming more interested in seeing with their eyes than invading Earth.

The Zog maintained its silence about the limitations of a future therapy, that it could only be administered before birth and even that treatment approach remained only hypothetical. Zooban researchers were performing gene modification in blastocysts, but for some unknown reason, the blastocysts weren't surviving. Some experts speculated that the altered genes would never work in Zoobans. However, if that were the case, the scientists wanted to know why—perhaps they could figure out a way to overcome the obstacle. Perhaps other genetic differences not yet identified played a role.

Ziglo couldn't believe his buddy Zeglo had been put in charge of the crime unit in District 497623. "How did you manage that?" he asked Zeglo as they sat at a small table in the back of Zolobob's store eating zoofeejee. "Nothing personal, but I didn't think you had it in you."

"Yeah, I have to admit, I'm surprised myself," said Zeglo. "Maybe they'd give the job to someone like you. You ran a tight operation. But me? I'm near the bottom of the aptitude scale, and, well, I'm not exactly the slimmest officer in the unit."

Zeglo bit off a corner of a zoofeejee. "These are excellent," he said as he chewed. "I think you found yourself a good female there, Ziglo. She sounds pretty hot, and she makes delectable zoofeejee."

"Yeah, I eat these all the time. Supposed to help with weight control, but I don't know. Eat enough of them, and you get fat," said Ziglo, chuckling. "I put on a little extra weight myself."

Zeglo took another bite of the pastry.

"So what's it like at the top? I suppose you have to work longer hours?" asked Ziglo.

"Well, lots of meetings, lots of records to process. Actually, so far, it has been kind of boring. But I'm privy to a lot more confidential information."

"Really? When you and I were processors, they didn't tell us *anything*— seemed like we were always the last to know." Ziglo leaned back in his chair. "So, anything interesting about the Earth invasion you can tell your old partner?"

"Well, I'm starting to hear rumblings about moving up the timing. The Zog's getting nervous. They're saying the longer we wait, the greater chance that public unrest could throw off the mission. Some of the senior officials want to send a lot of infantry to Earth... and fast. But they need everyone to cooperate."

Though he still felt hungry, Zeglo moved his empty plate toward the center of the table.

"Yeah, it's getting a little unsettled out there. More and more people want those genes so they can see with their eyes," Zeglo said. "And, of course, the air and water aren't getting any cleaner around here.

Supposedly there's this underground movement that wants to employ more conservation," he said.

"That must have the Zog really jittery. Last thing they want is reduced consumption," said Ziglo pushing his plate away. "It's their ultimate nightmare."

"Exactly. Oh, and they want to retrieve that Zooban kid they dropped off on Earth. I don't understand what they think they'll learn from him. He's just one kid. I guess they also want to practice another Earth landing."

"Can I get you brave male warriors anything else?" said Zolobob as she arrived back at the table, twirling her long red hair with her finger.

"No thanks, sweet one," said Ziglo. "You can just give Zeglo the bill... now that he's at the helm of 497623."

"You know these are always on the house," said Zolobob sounding surprised.

"I know. I just enjoy giving old Zeg here a hard time."

Zeglo put his finger up to his ear to activate the receiver embedded near his cochlea. "I just got a call. They want me back at headquarters to process some shoplifting ring," he said. "This is the third time I've had to deal with this group. They're just bored teenagers."

"I know you need to go, but speaking of shoplifters, any idea what they might do with the Earthling they locked up?"

"No, haven't heard anything. But I don't think they'll let him go. Do you still visit him?"

"Yeah. I feel bad for him. He's just a bored, innocent kid."

"Unfortunately, he's just a harmless kid from another planet who can see. They're afraid he's going to wreak some kind of havoc."

"I think he'd behave just fine if they gave him some kind of life," said Ziglo as he stood up from the table. "Yeah, when it comes down to it, he's really not that different from the rest of us when we were his age."

Chapter 18

Zellie wasn't a virgin; she'd had sex with a few young Zooban males before. The relationships were never serious or long-lasting, but they were pleasurable flings typical of the encounters had by most young Zooban adults. Zellie always practiced birth control, inserting a small capsule inside her cervix that released a sperm-destroying chemical for forty-eight hours. The approach was safe and virtually 100 percent reliable for occasional sexual activity.

However, Zellie forbade herself to have intercourse with Doug. She wasn't taking any chances of being impregnated by the Earthling. She was convinced some crazy life form would emerge. Surely, the hybrid offspring would bring big problems. The child, if it survived, might be subjected to all the invasive experiments performed on Doug. Zellie was also concerned she'd be ostracized and locked away.

So instead of screwing during her hour-long visits, Doug and Zellie got naked, snorted some zing, and ran their fingers, tongues, and lips across each other's plump bodies. Sometimes, to keep Doug quiet so he wouldn't be heard by the guards, Zellie would gag him with a cloth sash. While it did muffle his moaning and groaning, the bondage made him even more excited. Often, toward the end of a visit, Zellie would pin Doug up to a wall and rub herself against him until they climaxed.

Because Zellie's visits were infrequent and brief, their intercourse-free sex was urgent and frenzied. Neither Zellie nor Doug grew bored; they were always wanting each other. The three-day wait for their next encounter seemed like an eternity to them. And when they did meet again, they went at each other with an intensity that no other relationship—Zooban or human—could otherwise sustain. It was ironic how two of the most oppressed beings on Zooba—an alien prisoner and a caregiver for orphans—were its most impassioned.

Doug eventually told Ziglo during one of his visits about his heated relationship with Zellie. Not only could he not contain himself from talking about the intense singular pleasure in his life, he also wanted to see what Ziglo thought about the tryst. Were he and Zellie potentially opening themselves up to big trouble if their relations were discovered by the authorities at the Zohag?

"She's all I think about, day and night. I mean, we're so in love. When she's gone, all I do is fantasize about her smell and the taste of her," said Doug, sitting on the edge of his chair during one of Ziglo's visits.

Embarrassed, Ziglo interrupted him. "OK, Doug, OK. I get the picture. That's great that you make each other happy."

"But I'm scared. What if the guards find out and tell the Zog? Then what?"

"I know, Doug. I know. You and Zellie are in potentially dangerous, uncharted territory," said Ziglo, standing up from his chair. Doug, unconsciously mimicking Ziglo, stood up as well. Ziglo began slowly walking around Doug's room, running his fingers through his beard, trying to imagine the possible outcomes if the pair got caught in the heat of romance. He speculated that Doug probably had less to lose because he was already incarcerated indefinitely. Zellie would likely suffer the most. Being more paranoid and reactionary than ever, the Zog might lock her up. On the hand, maybe they wouldn't care. No one was getting hurt. Given that Zellie was all Doug had and might ever have in his life, Ziglo wouldn't tell him to stop having relations with her—not that Doug or Zellie would have the will to break off their sexual activities.

"Look, Doug, all I can say right now is to keep it cool," said Ziglo as he stopped pacing. "Don't change Zellie's visiting routine. Don't let her bring in any unusual packages—just the zoofeejee. And, whatever you do, don't get Zellie pregnant. That would certainly be big trouble."

"I know," said Doug. "Zellie's careful about that. She won't let me get inside her."

Ziglo cringed. "OK, Doug! I don't need to know the gory details!"

"Oh, sorry." Doug sat back down on the side of his bed.

The last thing Ziglo wanted to be was a prison inmate's sex advisor, but, alas, here he was counseling a young incarcerated alien male with a raging libido. The stakes were high for this hard-luck Earthling and his Zooban lover, and they had no one else to confide in. Ziglo felt obliged to help when he could.

However, he was having enough trouble navigating the progeny-bearing issue with Zolobob. She had a strong desire to conceive—a recurring topic of discussion she'd often bring up after their coital relations—but Ziglo was firmly against it. Though they had plenty of resources to raise a family, it didn't make sense to Ziglo with all the environmental problems plaguing the planet. Why bring more consumers into the world when consumption was jeopardizing its existence? Luckily for Ziglo, Zolobob tired considerably after their lovemaking and never put up much of a fight. And deep down she knew he was right—the last thing Zooba needed was more Zoobans.

One night after Zolobob had drifted off into a deep sleep, Ziglo lay awake, imagining what it might be like for Doug and Zellie if they were able to live normal lives—have a home and a family and run a vending operation like Zolobob and many other Zoobans did. As much as he wished it for them, he knew normalcy would never be possible for a Zooban-Earthling couple. He could only imagine what difficulties it would bring to them if they had progeny; their kids might be considered freaks, or at least different, by other youth.

Then he wondered whether a Zooban-Earthling progeny would be able to see. Could copies of those four human vision-enabling genes be passed down? He calculated there was a one in sixteen chance that a Zooban-human offspring would get a copy of all four human genes. It was more likely that only some, but not all, of the gene copies would be inherited by a child. But maybe the progeny would see if it got three or even just two of the human copies. Had Zooban scientists experimented with a subset of the four? What might researchers have already learned that they weren't disclosing? Maybe Doug and Zellie would have to have several children to conceive one with vision. Or scientists could conduct in vitro fertilization until they created a blastocyst with all four human copies. His mind started racing. Ziglo's curiosity was piqued, but many questions remained.

Then he had an exciting revelation. If the offspring of a Zooban-Earthling baby could see, then the challenge of endowing Zoobans with vision would be conquered—sort of. The answer would be in cross-species conception. A spooky idea—yes. Would these slight genetic differences *really* lead to some bizarre mutant progeny? Ziglo wasn't a scientist, but he knew enough to hypothesize, somewhat comfortably, that they probably wouldn't. Zoobans and humans were too much alike. Their offspring likely wouldn't be *that* strange. Even if Zellie had a baby who couldn't see but was otherwise healthy, the child would at least be proof that humans and Zoobans could successfully procreate. It would provide hope that with a little more research, eyesight might be possible for Zoobans someday.

Chapter 19

The crowd for the tenth-annual fundraising concert for the Iowa Environmental Defense Fund was to be Rhodopsin's biggest audience ever, and they had Marcy to thank for recommending them as the event's opening musical act. The outdoor gathering held in late September at Water Works Park typically attracted more than three thousand people from around the state who paid the fifty dollar admission to support the IEDF's educational and lobbying efforts. The group's assistant director heard Marcy deliver a compelling speech about pollution caused by the state's pig farms during regional high school debate finals the previous spring and asked her to be one of the event's speakers.

Marcy usually wasn't intimidated when speaking publicly but was awed by the large crowd that became quiet as she wheeled herself on the stage and up to the microphone. With thick blonde curls and a light-blue flowery sundress, she looked more like a child prodigy performer who might suddenly emerge from her wheelchair to tap dance than a fierce advocate for the animals and the planet.

She waited while an audio-visual tech sprinted out to adjust the mike down to her level. She couldn't believe the number of people on blankets and lawn chairs who had gathered on the large grassy section of the bucolic park on this warm, overcast Sunday in early fall. Marcy hadn't spoken to an audience of more than a few hundred, and those were mostly kids at school assemblies. She was self-conscious about her chair. Would people really listen to her or just think she was some kind of handicapped freak show?

Marcy had practiced her speech twice a day for the last week, and since it was derived from her debate remarks, which she had memorized well a few months ago, she could practically recite it backward. She knew the best thing to do at this point was to get on with it.

"Good afternoon, IEDF supporters. Thank you for being here today to learn about the many problems that plague Iowa's environment and the many ways you can help. I am honored for the opportunity to speak to you about the horrible pollution caused by Iowa's factory pig farms."

Marcy looked across the quiet crowd—most people were on blankets and lawn chairs, all were looking toward the stage—as she brushed her hair from her face, amazed that they had given her their full attention. She continued.

"When you ate breakfast this morning, you probably had a few slices of bacon on your plate. My family did. My mom makes it crispy, just the way she and my dad like it. But after learning about Iowa's pork industry earlier this year, I stopped eating bacon. I'm making progress in getting my parents to stop, but they're kind of stubborn."

Marcy heard chuckles. She paused, still incredulous that the mass of people, stretching back for more than a hundred yards to the edge of a wooded area, were all listening to her. She felt a sudden rush of empowerment. She knew the crowd was tuned in, and she was determined to drive home the remainder of her three-minute speech.

The five members of Rhodopsin, a skinny bunch of bushy-haired, high school boys dressed in dark jeans and T-shirts, stood stage right behind a curtain that cut them off from the crowd. Though they could see and hear Marcy from their vantage point, they weren't listening much because they were anxiously anticipating their performance after she finished. Retina Boy tapped his foot nervously as he thought about the band's short set, second-guessing the three songs they had chosen for the gig. Was "Purple Haze" too hard for this largely adult crowd? Were "Wish You Were Here" and "After the Goldrush" too mellow? How well would the sound system project to the people way in back? Retina Boy was spooked by how quiet the crowd had gotten while Marcy was speaking. This wasn't a party or a dance where half the people were busy eating, drinking, and screaming at each other above the music. These people were really paying attention! Apparently, they heard Marcy just fine.

"Iowa's pork industry generates more than $7 billion in revenue every year. And factory farmers raise nearly twenty-one million pigs, which dwarfs Iowa's human population of only three million. But what's most frightening about this industry is that it produces *nine billion* gallons of manure, which contaminate the Des Moines and Racoon Rivers running through this very park over there."

As Marcy pointed to her left to toward the Des Moines River, she heard a plopping noise on the canopy above the stage. As she continued with her speech, the sound of the light thuds on canvas persisted, becoming steady and more frequent. Some people near the front of the stage looked skyward. Others began to pack up their belongings.

As Marcy concluded, imploring people to write to their state legislators about the pig industry's disregard for the environment, a heavy rain began to fall on the park. There was no lightning, thunder, or even wind—the deluge of water came straight down. Mayhem ensued as the crowd ran for cover. All Marcy and Rhodopsin could do was watch the rainfall and people scatter as the event ended abruptly. The band never played a single note.

No one in the Pullman's van spoke as it followed a long line of traffic out of the park. "I can't believe it. They weren't forecasting rain," Meg muttered to her husband after he turned left onto Grand Avenue. Marc just shook his head. No one else responded. Marcy and the band members struggled to express their shock and disappointment.

A few minutes later, Retina Boy turned to Marcy. "You were basically the whole event," he said. "You were great. Everyone was really listening."

"Thanks," she said, putting her hand on his knee then quickly pulling it away, afraid that his eyes would turn indigo and freak everyone out. "You know, all those people could really make a difference if they wanted to."

"You mean if they all contacted their government officials?"

"Well, yeah, that would be good," Marcy replied. "But imagine if everyone there today just stopped eating bacon and pork. I mean, that would be so cool—for the environment *and* the pigs."

She was tempted to launch into a rant about how awfully pigs are treated, kept in gestation crates so small they can't turn around. There were also downer dairy cows, whose male calves are taken away to become veal. There were male chicks dumped alive into grinders because they didn't produce eggs. And all of these horrors happened in Iowa! But she knew this was not the time or place for factory farm proselytizing with everyone bummed by the rainout. At the same time, she felt something had to be done. But what? She began to doubt that her speech made a difference; would people change their eating habits simply because some overachieving, high school kid told them to?

Marcy threatened to go vegan a few times before but had a hard time envisioning what she'd eat. Her meat-and-potatoes parents would probably not react well; they'd never let her eat just pasta and salads for dinner. School lunches would be a challenge; the cafeteria usually offered only burgers, chicken, fish, and occasionally meat-and-cheese lasagna and pizza. A local vegetarian group had been fighting for more plant-based options, but the school sent out a survey to parents, which revealed that virtually no one wanted them. And what would she do when she went out with Rhodopsin for their beloved pepperoni and cheese pizza at University Zah's after their gigs? But then again, how could she expect people to change their eating habits if she herself was still eating animals that were raised inhumanely and polluted the environment?

At her family dinner table later that night, Marcy couldn't bring herself to eat the lamb chops her dad had made on the outdoor grill. The thought of putting the cooked flesh of a baby animal in her mouth repulsed her. It was as if some switch in her head for meat-eating had suddenly flipped into the off position. Instead, she ate a salad, green beans, and baked potato with sour cream. Giving up eggs and milk—especially cheese—would take some effort. But two months later, Marcy had sworn off animal products entirely. No one, not even her parents, was particularly surprised. As Retina Boy told his parents, "Going vegan is such a Marcy thing to do."

Marcy's mother spent considerable time at Campbell's Nutrition, the local health food store, learning about the plethora of animal-free protein alternatives she could feed her daughter, including tofu, texturized vegetable protein, wheat gluten, beans, and nuts. They even sold vegan cheeses, a couple of which her family agreed weren't all that bad.

Though Retina Boy completely understood and respected Marcy's rationale for going vegan, he himself lacked interest in giving up meat. Like Marcy had, he couldn't imagine making such a radical change in his diet. The will to do it just had never been there for him.

However, a few months later an unexpected call from Danny led to a profound change in the way Retina Boy felt about animals.

"I know this is going to sound weird, but we're going to put Mongo down this afternoon. He's really sick from the leukemia, and my parents said I should ask you if you want to be there," Danny said somberly. "The cat really liked you, even more than I think he liked us. The vet's doing it at the house, and my dad said he'd even give you a ride over here if you need one."

In his eighteen years on the planet, Retina Boy had never lost anything or anyone special; death was an abstraction for him. Though he felt apprehensive about witnessing the Pullman's beloved pet being euthanized—he figured it would be very sad, perhaps even frightening to witness an animal being put down—he felt obliged since Danny and his parents seemed to really want him there.

In recent days, Mongo had become only a shadow of the big gray tabby he once was. He'd thinned considerably, and his coat was dull and matted down. He'd stopped eating and staggered when he walked. He spent most of the day underneath a coffee table in the back of the living room.

When Retina Boy arrived at the Pullman's after having gotten a ride over from his father, everyone stood near the long wooden table in the dining room. Retina Boy stood next to Danny's father. "He's gone downhill quickly over the last week," he whispered to Retina Boy.

As he began tearing up, Marc Pullman, a tall man with long arms and large, thick hands, went to the living area to retrieve the cat. When he returned with Mongo in his arms, he put the cat on a large white towel covering most of the dining room table. Meg stood in the corner crying with her hands covering her face. When the family decided to adopt a cat, Meg insisted on adopting one with feline leukemia because most cats with the disease were abandoned in shelters or destroyed.

The vet, a young thin woman dressed in dark-blue scrubs with her blonde hair pulled back in a ponytail, explained that she'd be giving the cat two injections: first a sedative, then a euthanizing solution. The Pullmans and Retina Boy took turns petting Mongo and saying goodbye while the vet waited in the kitchen. Retina Boy recalled how startled he was when the big cat first jumped up on his lap during practice, but how wonderful and comforting it felt to have this warm, furry, affectionate creature make him his friend. Maybe Mongo liked blind kids. It was as if the cat had adopted *him*.

Meg stroked Mongo's head as the vet administered the first injection into the cat's back leg. Mongo lay on his side, motionless, content, as if he knew that his suffering was coming to an end. Everyone in the room held their breath as they watched the vet give the second injection.

Though Retina Boy couldn't see the process, he sensed a change in the energy in the room after the second injection, the fading of Mongo's life force. But shortly after, he felt something replace it—an infusion of serenity. Retina Boy felt lighter, as if less encumbered by gravity. These new feelings were remarkable to him. Yes, he felt sad for the loss of the wonderful creature that had befriended him. But the cat's death was not all the doom and gloom he had expected it to be. Though he had a difficult time making sense of it, there was beauty and grace in Mongo's departure. It felt more like an exchange than a loss. Something extraordinary was happening. Yes, this beautiful animal had slipped away, but something was given back.

Retina Boy never talked about the experience of Mongo's death with anyone else. It felt too abstract and personal to share with anyone. He would never be the devout vegan that Marcy was, but he did become vegetarian a couple of weeks later. Mongo's death had taught him how precious and powerful life was, even for a cat.

Chapter 20

Zellie walked slowly away from the Zohag, hanging her head, feeling tremendous guilt for not having had sex with Doug. It was the first time since they'd been intimate that she hadn't had the desire; she had never turned him down before. She knew Doug would be an emotional mess for the next few days, wondering if something terribly wrong was happening between them. He'd fear that she would abandon him forever. Zellie had tried to explain that her lack of interest was temporary, that she just wasn't feeling well, which was true.

At first, Doug was incredulous, but his shock quickly morphed into anger. After a few minutes of Zellie's reassuring pleas that everything was OK, he'd pounded his fists in his bed, yelling, "Why? Why? Why?" He'd been like a five-year-old having a tantrum. He cried in her arms before she left.

However, Doug's emotional state was the least of Zellie's problems. She knew with little doubt she was pregnant. Her menstrual cycle had never been this late, and her nausea and vomiting were likely morning sickness.

"If you and Doug have a baby who can see, that will change Zooba forever," Ziglo had said to her one afternoon a few months earlier outside the Zohag after her visit with Doug. He had been so determined to talk to her about his idea, he had contacted one of the guards to let him know when she was visiting so he could be certain to meet her to present his revelation. "I know it's risky. I'm no genetics genius, but I think there's a good chance your baby would have vision. Not only would it get you and Doug out of this torturous separation, it might convince the authorities to postpone or reconsider the Earth invasion. Or at least it would distract everyone from it. At least I think it would."

Ziglo had explained that all of Zooba's attention would turn to Doug. He said that females from all over the planet would want to be impregnated by him, hoping their progeny would see. At first, Zellie was amused by the thought that the petulant one-eyed human male with an insatiable sex drive would become the planet's prized stud. Ziglo's logic had sounded so convincing at the time, enough for her to begin having unprotected sex with Doug. But after having had more time to think about it, Zellie only imagined that their life would go horribly wrong. The more she considered Ziglo's hypothesis, the more it seemed improbable. What if the baby didn't see, or, worse yet, it had deformities? Not only would she and Doug suffer public mocking and embarrassment, it would be a hellacious life for their child.

Zing withdrawals were exacerbating her turmoil. She hardly ate or slept. She'd been off the powder for more than a week for the sake of her baby's health. It was the longest she'd abstained from the chemical since early adolescence. While zing wasn't nearly as addictive or dangerous as most recreational chemicals, it was nonetheless a habit difficult to break. Zellie knew it would take another week or two until she'd be completely withdrawn. But then she'd still have the pregnancy to contend with—and at some point, she'd no longer be able to keep it a secret.

Putting the child up for adoption made little sense given her work as a caretaker; it would be sadly ironic for her to be caring for parentless kids, but at the same time not having the gumption to care for her own child.

Terminating the pregnancy would have been the easy way out. No baby—no problem. The Zog was tolerant of abortions, especially for children who would otherwise be born to parents without much consuming potential. But Zellie felt it heartless to just off the developing child, never giving it a fighting chance.

When Zellie got a about a mile away from her apartment, a steady rain began to fall—a highly unusual phenomenon with most of the planet being arid and smoggy. Most Zoobans nearby ran for cover, their footsteps squishing and sloshing as they scurried away from the unsheltered walking path that bisected the commercial sector. Zellie's first instinct was to run, but the rain felt refreshing on her face and skin, so she slowed her pace to take in as much of the unlikely shower as she could. She pulled off her smog mask for the first time in several weeks. Rain or not, Zellie liked her time in between destinations—being neither here nor there. While she usually enjoyed her visits with Doug and felt obliged to provide at least a modicum of stability and love to young orphans, she was content when she was alone outdoors, where no one was screaming, crying, or begging.

The rain persisted for the remainder of her journey home, and as she approached her building, she felt less overwhelmed by her predicament. She felt cleansed. She recalled a comment, almost a plea, from Ziglo, which began to resonate with her again.

"If you don't have his baby, Doug's just going to sit in the Zohag and slowly rot away while you watch him," he had said. "Meanwhile, not only will Zooba continue to fall apart, it will take Earth down with it."

Chapter 21

When Marcy called Retina Boy to ask him to come over to her house, he was sitting on the floor of his basement putting new strings on his acoustic Martin in preparation for Rhodopsin's New Year's Eve show that evening at Java Joe's. The guitar still played brightly, but replacing the strings seemed a good way to get the new year off to a fresh start. While the coffeehouse wasn't likely to draw a huge crowd—mostly because it didn't serve any alcohol—Retina Boy appreciated the numerous gigs that the owners had given Rhodopsin, especially in the band's early days, so he wanted to put on a top-notch performance for its patrons.

As he walked to her house, Retina Boy wondered why Marcy asked him to stop whatever he was doing to come by. She had assured him that nothing bad had happened. She was fine, and no one in her family, including their cat, a massive white Maine coon named Yeti, had died or been diagnosed with some horrible terminal disease.

"So I know I'm going to see you later at Java Joe's, but I just couldn't wait to tell you," Marcy said, sitting alongside Retina Boy on the edge of her bed. "I got a full scholarship to the UC Berkeley astronomy program. Tuition. Room. Board. And they have a really cool research center for searching for extraterrestrial life." Marcy took in a deep breath and began to cry. She put her hands over her mouth so no one else in the house could hear her.

"What's the matter? That's so cool!" Retina Boy said, putting his arm around her and squeezing tightly. "I mean, that's what you wanted. And a full scholarship!" Though he wasn't expecting any kind of news in particular when she had called that afternoon, her acceptance to Berkeley wasn't a surprise at all. Every college she'd applied to accepted her and most offered generous scholarships. He knew Berkeley was at or near the top of her list.

More than anything, Marcy was scared—scared to leave Iowa, her parents, Retina Boy. She had made a safe, comfortable life for herself, surrounded by people who supported her and took care of her. Des Moines was a small, tightly knit community. Deep down, Marcy knew she would be OK, but the reality of moving almost two thousand miles away to a place where she knew no one was overwhelming.

The admissions counselor at Berkeley had assured her that "everything will be just fine" regarding accommodating her mobility needs if she attended the school. None ever dared admit it, but many candidate schools envisioned Marcy as their own Stephen Hawking–like character, a disabled cosmology genius. An attractive young woman in a wheelchair studying the heavens would be quite compelling from a public relations standpoint.

While he felt bad about her being so upset, Retina Boy was in denial about the possible impact of Marcy's departure on him and their relationship. She'd be around until July or August, which to him seemed a long way off. Why worry about it now? It was difficult for him to imagine what it would be like to be separated from Marcy for an extended time. They'd seen each other most every day for the last few years. But being without her was a concept he just couldn't wrap his head around.

Retina Boy also wasn't concerned about Marcy adapting to life at Berkeley. She'd be in her element among all those bright, ambitious students. When she was faced with an obstacle or denied something she wanted, she was a force to be reckoned with, often unwilling to take "no" for an answer. He pitied the poor souls who might try to get in her way. It was best to be on Marcy's side in any argument or dispute. The new people in her life would learn that soon enough.

After Marcy calmed down, Retina Boy stood up, stretched, and decided to change the conversation to the program at Berkeley to reignite her excitement about going there. "So, how do they actually look for alien life?" he asked as he plopped himself back down on the end of the bed opposite where she sat. "Do they use telescopes?"

"Well, sort of." Marcy blew her nose in a tissue. "They're looking at radio and light waves and electromagnetic activity in space."

"Wow, cool."

"Yeah, it is pretty cool. But there are billions of galaxies. Some are billions of light years away. So I'm not sure what happens if you do find something or someone."

"Maybe you could friend them on Facebook," said Retina Boy with a grin.

Marcy picked up the box of tissues and lobbed it at him. "Great idea, Einstein. Maybe you should go to Berkeley and lead the cosmology program." Retina Boy retrieved the box and tossed it back at her. "So what if you never find any intelligent life?" he said. "What if you go your whole career and find nothing at all? Wouldn't that suck?"

"Yeah, it would suck." The thought of that ominous eventuality hadn't occurred to Marcy before. She felt a chill. "Well, hopefully we'd learn more about the universe—or all the universes—and all the stars and planets," she replied, trying to find consolation in the thought of coming up empty in a career-long quest for alien life.

"If anyone can find life out there in outer space, you can," said Retina Boy, standing up and trying to end the conversation on an upbeat note. "Well, I gotta get ready for Java Joe's. We're picking you up at seven thirty."

"Wait, before you go I have kind of a present for you—well, they're actually for both of us," Marcy said, reaching for a small paper bag on the night stand beside her bed. She pulled out two bracelets made of a thin rope material. "I got us friendship bracelets when I was out shopping with my mom. Yours is this beautiful turquoise color, just like your eyes. Mine is bright blue. But you have to wear it forever. You can never take it off."

"Really, not even in the shower?"

"Nope, the lady at the craft store said they're water resistant. They'll be OK in the shower. Now give me one of your wrists so I can tie it on."

Retina Boy extended his left arm. "Is this like we're getting married? Maybe I should talk to my lawyer first. You know, maybe we need a prenup."

"Don't be a prick," Marcy grumbled as she carefully tied the bracelet to his wrist. "I don't have a scissors here. You can cut off the ends or just leave them dangling."

"OK," said Retina Boy. "Do you think it looks good?"

"Yes, it's beautiful. Very fashionable."

"But, I don't want to look *fashionable*."

"Don't get worked up. Most people probably won't even notice it."

"OK," Retina Boy conceded. "I gotta get going."

After he left her house, Marcy put on her bracelet and then lay down on her bed to nap. She needed a rest; she'd be up late that night and was tired from the excitement of the news from Berkeley. Marcy fell asleep quickly and deeply. She dreamed vividly of flying in a jet to San Francisco on her way to school. It was a smooth flight, and all the crew and attendants were doting on her as if she were a celebrity astronomer. Somehow, the plane ended up in space among thousands of bright, shimmering stars. She felt weightless, free of her chair, and gasped at the sight of a supernova exploding in a rainbow of colors off in the distance. It was as if the heavenly show was being put on just for her.

Marcy awoke feeling refreshed. She recalled dreaming something about flying through space but couldn't recall the details. Regardless, a dream about the cosmos seemed like a good omen to her. She was ready to celebrate the start of what she was sure would be an incredible year.

Chapter 22

Jenny Manheim was glad she'd followed the farmer's advice. "You'd better
wear jeans and tall rubber boots. It's a decent walk, and it's a bit sloppy,"
Fred Adams had said to her on the phone. "With this warm rainy spell, the
ground isn't frozen the way it normally is this time of year." Having grown up
in Evanston, Illinois, a Chicago suburb, Jenny had never set foot on a serious
farm. But now she was traipsing through a vast field of mud. She knew she'd
likely never cover anything that would make it to the front page, but she was
still hoping to occasionally write juicy crime stories: shootings, exploding meth
labs, child molesters. Perhaps it was only fitting that her first story would take
her to a farm. She was in Iowa, after all.

Several of the Des Moines Register newsroom staff were covering the
disappearance of Doug Anderson. The young blind musician, also known
as Retina Boy, had gone missing a few days earlier. So the assignment
editor, Kyle, gave the "mud circle" story to his new intern from Iowa State.
"I'm sure it's just bullshit," he said to Jenny, who sat in front of his desk
while he typed on his computer keyboard. "But it will be good practice
for you. Get some quotes from the farmer. Get some photos. I don't know,
maybe we'll run it in the local section on Sunday to give people a light
change of pace from the missing kid."

Jenny couldn't tell if the balding, pudgy, middle-aged journalist in
a maroon cardigan was normally this snarky or if he was just trying to

impress his young female charge. Maybe after working in the newsroom at the Des Moines Register for twenty years, Kyle was what one became.

The mud circle was more of an oval in shape but remarkably large—about a third of an acre long according to Adams. The oval was nothing more than a depression about a foot deep in the soggy earth. Jenny slowly walked around the oval—with every step making a loud squishing sound—as Adams looked on, about ten yards below its southern edge. Most striking to her was the uniform depth of the depression; the bottom of it was flat and level with several small puddles. It looked as if the ground had been dug to put in a huge wading pool. Jenny couldn't imagine how this vast recess in the earth could have been made without the orchestrated effort of several people for many hours who knew what they were doing—at least when it came to digging holes. And according to Adams, he had just noticed it a couple of mornings ago. There had been no hint of anyone or anything out in the field. If there had been footprints nearby, they'd likely been washed out by the rain.

"Thanks, Mr. Adams, for letting me take a look as this. It's quite something," Jenny said after returning from surveying and photographing the mysterious oval. "I have a few more questions, if you don't mind."

"OK," he replied, taking his hands out of the pockets of his red down vest and folding his arms. He wasn't tall, but he was thin and broad shouldered. His hands were thick and so calloused that they felt reptilian when she shook his hand. His grip was formidable; Jenny imagined he could crush her hand to pieces if he wasn't careful. If he had any hair left, it was covered by a Cubs baseball cap. His stoic expression never changed during the interview. For all Jenny knew, he hadn't cracked a smile in years.

"So I am just curious, Mr. Adams. Why did you call us instead of the police?"

Adams shrugged his shoulders and looked out over the field. "No big crime, I guess. Well, maybe trespassing," he replied, shifting his boots in the mud. "Wife said the newspaper ought to get a look. She's out grocery shopping right now."

The farmer turned to Jenny, who nodded as she jotted a note in her steno pad. Adams couldn't believe the newspaper would hire such a young woman to do its reporting. With her long blonde hair and tiny stature—she couldn't have been more than four ten or eleven, he surmised—she looked more like a high school cheerleader.

What Adams didn't tell Jenny is that he was thinking about putting the farm up for sale and retiring. Also, he'd been having issues with his short-term memory. He'd gotten lost driving home one afternoon the previous week and was worried he was going senile. Maybe he was getting Alzheimer's. He was afraid that if law enforcement got involved, they'd see that he was losing it and lock him away in a nursing home.

Jenny took in a big breath and exhaled as she looked back out over the field. "So neither you nor your wife has seen or heard anything suspicious? Nothing unusual?"

"Nope. Been real quiet. Except for the rain. Had a lot of rain."

As Jenny walked back to her car, she didn't feel convinced of anything about the mud circle. She found it hard to believe that Adams was behind a hoax or wanting of attention. He didn't have much to say about the strange phenomenon. If anything, he was unsettled by it.

Back at the newsroom, Jenny sat at another reporter's desk to use his computer while he was out. She didn't have her own work space yet. To the right of the keyboard was a one-page profile of Retina Boy. It included a school yearbook photo, his address, height, weight, hair and eye color, and other miscellaneous facts. Jenny was drawn to his aquamarine eyes. They were beautiful but at the same time a little spooky. It looked as if someone had Photoshopped them in. Coincidentally, she and Retina Boy shared a birthday, June 3rd, but he was a few years younger, having been born in 1996.

A paragraph of text at the bottom of the page read: "No known drug use. No criminal record or history of violence. Lives with both parents.

No siblings. Good grades. Musician. University of Iowa in the fall. Girlfriend (disabled)."

Jenny had heard during an editorial staff briefing the day before that authorities normally wouldn't get too excited about the disappearance of an eighteen-year-old male, especially if he'd been gone just a few days. But given that Doug Anderson was blind, had a clean record, and didn't drive, made his case particularly unusual. Also, according to his parents, when they went to wake him up in the morning for school, he was gone without trace. He hadn't even taken his wallet. While the parents were suspects at this juncture, the detectives couldn't establish any motive—all the family's neighbors and friends insisted the Andersons adored their only child—and there wasn't anything like a life insurance policy for them to collect on upon his death.

After doing some background research on Adams and his wife, Jenny searched the internet and a media database for information about crop circles in Iowa. She couldn't come up with anything like a mud circle; most of the reports were on phenomena that had occurred in crops and grass fields. However, one brief crop circle story from a Des Moines television station caught her attention because of its date: June 4, 1996, the day after Doug Anderson was born. It occurred to her that the crop circle could have been made the day he was born. Jenny found the coincidence mildly compelling but wasn't sure what exactly to make of it.

While Jenny was pleased that Kyle ran her story—a photo with two paragraphs of copy—she was not happy with the headline: "Mudhenge Discovered in Farmer's Field." She felt it was condescending to Adams, though she admitted to herself that after all was said and done, the mud circle was likely a hoax, somebody's strange idea for a joke. There simply wasn't a better explanation for it.

Chapter 23

Retina Boy surmised he'd been hospitalized, perhaps because of a serious illness or accident. He'd been on his back for what seemed like days, too groggy to sit upright. But surprisingly, no one had come to visit him, at least that he could remember. There had been no sign of Marcy, his friends from Rhodopsin, or his parents. He couldn't even recall having been examined by any doctors or nurses. Occasionally, he heard noises, some movement or walking outside of his room. Perhaps he heard some muffled conversation, but he couldn't be sure. He faintly recalled drinking some type of broth from a bowl, but maybe that was just a dream. His whole body ached a little, but slowly, he was feeling better.

Eventually, he stayed awake for an hour or two at a time. He realized he wore a one-piece garment, essentially a jumpsuit, made of an ultrathin fabric, like a single layer of gauze. A thin band of what felt to him like hard rubber was wrapped around his left ankle.

At one point, Retina Boy got up from the bed and explored his room. He estimated it to be only about ten by fifteen feet. He ran his hands along the walls and floor, knocking on them lightly with his knuckles. They felt like hard plastic or rubber with thin ridges. He couldn't detect any odors. Usually when he was indoors, he could smell the mildew or chemicals from carpets and curtains, or the powerful cleaning products often used in public buildings.

Ultimately, he found a sink, two chairs, and some sort of metal receptacle, which he presumed was a toilet. He didn't feel an urgent need to go, but nonetheless peed in it for a considerably long time. After he finished, it made a quick whooshing sound, apparently flushing his urine. As mundane as his discovery of the toilet was, Retina Boy felt satisfaction in having found something familiar. The brief, unremarkable excursion around his room left him exhausted, so he went back to his bed, lay down, and sank into another deep sleep.

At what seemed to be a day or two day later, he mustered enough energy to search the room for a door or window. He found two long, narrow vertical seams in a wall, but no handle or latch.

Retina Boy thought about yelling or banging on a wall to see if he could get someone's attention. He heard noise on the other side of the wall adjacent to his bed, as if someone were moving around, but intuitively, he thought that trying to get somebody's attention seemed like an imprudent thing to do. He had no idea where he was or why he was locked up, but he felt more and more anxious, like he was in some type of danger. Maybe someone was looking for him, and he'd be rescued. Maybe it made sense to lay low until help arrived. But why in the world would anyone want to kidnap him? If he was being held captive by some type of sexual predator or deviant, wouldn't the person have molested him, or worse, by now?

The next time he woke up, there was a warm bowl of broth on a table at the foot of his bed. It came without a tray, spoon, or, to his disappointment, oyster crackers. As he sipped the concoction, it reminded him of miso but with a sweet yet medicinal aftertaste. The soup wasn't exactly tasty, but with his appetite coming back, it satisfied him.

Retina Boy's predicament reminded him of the novel *Papillon* he loved in tenth grade. In the story, a fugitive wrongly accused of murder was locked up in solitary confinement for several years in some god-awful penal colony in French Guinea. After being recaptured from several daring escapes, Papillion was ultimately sequestered to Devil's Island. Not to be deterred, he eventually made his way off the island in old age by riding the rip current out to sea on a bag of coconuts.

Unlike Papillon, Retina Boy wasn't living in a damp, filthy cell made of stone, eating bugs to survive. The twin-size bed in Retina Boy's cell was actually more comfortable than the lumpy mattress he used at home. As he regained his strength, it became more and more disconcerting not to know where he was or why he was being held captive. He wondered if he'd gone wacko. Would he even know if he'd gone crazy?

Chapter 24

At first, he thought he was dreaming, but as Retina Boy sat up in bed, he had no doubt the soft moaning emanated from the other side of the wall. He also heard a rhythmic banging and bouncing. Was someone being tortured? The thought of the possibility gave him a chill. He noticed that the sound was louder toward the top of the wall, so he stood up on his bed, and reached up with his hand and found a screen made of a light mesh material. He felt a light draft flowing from it.

Just a couple of seconds after the noise stopped, he heard someone let out a deep, loud sigh, followed by an equally loud "Shhhh!" from someone else, perhaps a girl. He quickly pulled his hand away from the screen, afraid he'd be noticed by whomever was on the other side. After the female giggled, a short unintelligible conversation ensued for the next couple of minutes. Then silence.

Retina Boy was relieved by the likelihood that what he had heard was not torture but a sexual encounter. He felt safer, at less risk of being in physical danger. People were having sex; they weren't killing one another. However, the romantic activity in the adjacent room did little to shed light on what was happening to him. It only perplexed him more. He found it difficult to feel calm or hopeful with so much uncertainty. Exhausted from the excitement, he lay back down on his bed and quickly fell asleep.

Upon waking a few hours later, he was determined to contact whomever was on the other side. He felt the need to be proactive. He stood up below the screen and tapped with his fingers on the wall next to it.

He heard no response, so he tapped a little louder.

"Hello?" came from the other side of the wall.

"Hello," said Retina Boy.

"What?"

"Hello," Retina Boy repeated more loudly.

"Hold on," said Doug, quickly retrieving a chair from the other side of the room so he could stand closer to the vent where the voice was coming from. "Can you hear me better now?" he said, projecting his voice toward the screen.

"Yes, much better," said Retina Boy. "Where the hell am I? Where are we?"

"We're in the Zohag. Don't you know that?"

"No. What's the Zohag? Is it like jail?

"Yes! I can't believe you don't know where you are?" said Doug, excited by the contact with another inmate. At the same time, he was annoyed by his ignorance.

"But why am I here? I didn't do anything?"

"The Zog doesn't care. They're ruthless."

"The Zog?" asked Retina Boy, mystified by the conversation. "What the hell is a Zog?"

"Yeah, the Zog," answered Doug in frustration. Growing more impatient, he wasn't sure what to say or ask next. He figured this other inmate was mentally disturbed or brain injured. The guy had issues. "So, what's your name?" he asked, trying to keep the conversation simple. "What district are you from?"

"I'm Doug. I'm from Iowa. Des Moines," replied Retina Boy. "How about you?"

"Wait. Your name is Doug?" exclaimed human Doug. "And you're from Iowa? Like the Iowa Hawkeyes?"

"Yeah," Retina Boy answered.

112

Doug's incredulity was palpable. He'd heard of the Hawkeyes while listening to Earth football broadcasts. He thought for a moment that he was losing his mind. The past few weeks had been stressful, with Zellie's loss of interest in sex, albeit temporary, and then learning that she was pregnant with his child. While Zellie and Ziglo had tried to reassure him that a baby with vision was his ticket out of the Zohag and into a more normal life, he was afraid, unable to process or rationalize the possible outcomes of Zellie's pregnancy. The contact with another inmate was just bringing him more anxiety and tension.

However, the pieces of the crazy puzzle of the conversation were quickly fitting together.

Though it wasn't publicized, Doug had heard recently from Ziglo that the Zog was planning to bring back the Zooban whom they brought to Earth—the Zooban who was swapped for him. They were in the throes of planning an invasion and occupation. They needed to examine the Zooban who'd been living on Earth to learn whatever they could about his life and health on the planet to ensure success of the plan.

"Holy shit," Doug muttered as he realized whom he was talking with.

"What was that?" said Retina Boy.

"Are you from Earth?" Doug asked matter-of-factly.

"Are you kidding me? What kind of question is that? Where the hell else would I be from? Mars?" Retina Boy rarely got sarcastic, but Doug's seemingly ridiculous question got under his skin.

Retina Boy's Mars reference threw Doug for a moment, he'd never heard of the place, but he continued on. "I bet you can't see with your eyes," he said.

"Yeah, that's right. I'm blind. How did you know? I mean, you can't see me, can you?"

"No, I can't. Not through this wall. But I know who you are."

"So tell me where the hell I am, and why I'm here," Retina Boy demanded. "I've been locked in here for days and haven't seen anyone."

"OK. This is going to sound completely crazy, but you have to believe me."

113

"OK," said Retina Boy, feeling some relief to finally learn what was happening to him.

"You're not really an Earthling. You're from the planet Zooba. Everyone from Zooba is blind. And that's where you are now." Doug heard footsteps passing by outside of his cell so he paused for a moment. Then he continued, speaking in a lower voice. "See, you and I were swapped when we were babies. I'm human. You're Zooban. I'm the real Doug."

"Riiiiiight," said Retina Boy, convinced now that he'd been sequestered in a mental institution. He was certain that the guy in the next room was loony tunes, completely off his rocker. He couldn't wait to tell Marcy about the wacky conversation he was having. But, he still had no explanation for why he was locked up in a nut house. He had no history of depression or mental illness. He was a happy, drug-free teenager with a girlfriend and a band!

Retina Boy's conversation, though it lasted only a few minutes, sapped all his energy, and he couldn't bear another word from his lunatic next-door neighbor. "Look, I got to go," he mumbled as he sat back down on his bed. While his lack of contact with the outside world remained perplexing, he began to wonder if he had an illness that made him extremely tired. Maybe he just needed to rest a few more days and then he'd be ready for discharge. Within seconds he fell, yet again, into a deep sleep.

Chapter 25

The Zog's retrieval of the young Zooban from Earth had led to the hasty formation of a few small committees for planning the invasion. One group of eleven officials was organized to process Retina Boy. Its primary tasks included a medical evaluation and interrogation to learn how well the Zooban had fared on the alien planet. While most of the members were scientists, Zeglo served as a facilitator to ensure that the committee moved expeditiously. Thanks to the criminal-processing system Ziglo had put in place before his retirement, Zeglo's district was the most efficiently run on the planet. That made Zeglo the top candidate to lead the committee.

While he didn't want to turn down the appointment, Zeglo was terrified by it. Running the district's criminal-processing operation was about as much responsibility as he could handle, and furthermore, he wasn't enthusiastic about the invasion, preferring instead to maintain the status quo.

So Zeglo had asked Ziglo to join the committee to assist as a consultant. "I don't need you to necessarily do much during the meetings, but it would be great if you could advise me strategically," he had pleaded to his friend and confidant. "Just let me know if I am doing the right thing—you know, guiding things in the right direction—and give me advice to get through any snags. You are much better at this kind of thing than I am."

To Ziglo, the idea of helping to prepare for the invasion was at first completely nauseating. However, after thinking about it, he relished the opportunity to meet the Zooban who had spent his life on Earth. What a great learning experience it would be—to hear about the alien land that hadn't been decimated by overconsumption. Was this planet in fact all it was cracked up to be? While he couldn't imagine preventing an invasion single-handedly, perhaps he could also plant some seeds to thwart it—or at least delay it until Zellie's baby was born.

In order to meet this Zooban boy from Earth, Ziglo's first goal was to convince the committee that the Earthling should be briefed before the formal interview process was initiated. "We have to remember that he's going to have no idea where he is let alone that he's Zooban," Ziglo had said during the team's first meeting. "We're going to get more information, and more reliable information if he has the opportunity to acclimate to his new situation. Undoubtedly, he'll be overwhelmed. Let's try to ease him into his new reality as best we can." The committee agreed and honored his request to conduct the briefing alone with the boy.

Retina Boy was startled by the sound of the sliding door in his cell retracting and closing. For the first time, he was aware of someone entering. He didn't feel danger, but Retina Boy sensed something strange about the visitor. The person was emitting a pulsing energy much different, much stronger from that of the people he knew. At the same time, it felt familiar. His visitor also had a pungent body odor, as if he hadn't bathed or changed his clothes for some time.

Ziglo remained only a few steps inside the cell, keeping his distance to minimize the fear he felt he must be eliciting. He cleared his throat. "Hello, Doug, my name is Ziglo. You are completely safe. I am here to help you... if I can."

Retina Boy could feel the visitor's energy intensify as he spoke and diminish when he stopped.

"OK," said Retina Boy, hesitantly. While his English appeared to be good, the visitor had an unfamiliar accent. He strongly enunciated consonants, sounding something like a German who had perhaps spent a lot of time around Americans.

As Ziglo explained to him where he was and why he was there, Retina Boy thought, "Uh-oh, here we go again." Unlike the other Doug who was high-strung and seemed as if he might snap at any moment, Ziglo exuded control and confidence. Remarkably, the rest of his story jibed with Doug's. As incredible as the story was, Ziglo was somewhat convincing. But Ziglo's description of the planned Earth invasion was also disturbing.

"Look," said Ziglo. "There's a lot more to talk about in preparation for your interview with the committee, but I know you're probably quite tired and still recovering from your journey to Zooba. So I will stop for now but will return again soon."

"Before you leave, I have a couple of questions," said Retina Boy. "If what you say is true and that I am Zooban and the real Doug is next door, then what is my real name? And for that matter, who are my real parents?"

"Well, you were born during the journey from Zooba to Earth, just before you were dropped off there. I don't know who your parents are—that was kept secret and may never be known—but you were named Zin, which is a type of flower now extinct. Many plant species are gone. We're getting close to the tipping point for our survival, because of the accelerating losses of plants and foliage."

"So my name is Zin, and I am named after a flower?"

"That's correct."

"Well, on Earth they call me Retina Boy. I prefer that, if that's OK," he said, surprised by his own willingness to go along with the improbable story he'd just been told by Ziglo.

"Sure. That's fine," said Ziglo, reaching into a satchel hanging from his shoulder. "And I brought you something to eat—a couple of zoofeejee—that my partner, Zolobob, made for you. They told me you were probably ready for solid food. But I'd take just a few bites to start, just to make sure your system can handle them."

"Whoa," said Retina Boy, feeling a burst of warm, soothing energy as the fellow Zooban reached his hand out with the bag of pastries. Retina Boy usually knew when someone on Earth was giving him something or extending their hand, but the vibe given off by Ziglo was like nothing he'd ever felt before. It was like a jolt of electricity.

After Ziglo left, Retina Boy lay awake in his bed unable to make sense of what was happening. On one hand, he refused to buy into the alien planet and invasion story. That seemed ridiculous. He was from Zooba? Really? But on the other hand, his experience with Ziglo was surreal. The guy—his voice, his smell, his energy—was like no one he'd met before. He also seemed sincere and believable.

Retina Boy had been missing Marcy's companionship in a big way—how great it would be for them just to go for a stroll in the park and talk. How he'd love to hear one of her rants about climate change and the destruction of the environment. And she was so excited to be going to Berkeley to study astronomy and search for extraterrestrial life. Hah! He'd found it first! He was allegedly the alien!

He felt he really needed her to help him understand what had just happened with this character named Ziglo. She'd be able to see the guy with her eyes and know what was going on, or at least have a good theory or two. Or maybe she'd think he'd completely lost his marbles. Maybe that was the problem. Maybe he had.

Retina Boy pulled one of the zoofeejee out of the bag. The pastry was still warm and had an enticing sweet aroma, like fresh pastry from back home. He bit off a corner. It tasted OK—like a cross between a bagel and croissant but with a chalky aftertaste. He got to the sweet filling with the second bite and ignoring Ziglo's suggestion to go slow with solid food he devoured the whole pastry.

Chapter 26

The mysterious disappearance of Retina Boy had been all over the local news for the last six weeks. Despite being grateful for the community's efforts to find their son, Peg and Peter Anderson were reluctant to talk with any media. The absence of clues confounded them as it did law enforcement. The Andersons presumed the worst and were particularly reticent to talk publicly after watching a television interview of a detective, who had said, matter-of-factly, "His remains could be in a field anywhere—we might never find them." Along with volunteer search teams, authorities had scoured virtually every park, empty field, vacant lot, and unsecured dumpster in Polk County but came up with nothing.

Jenny couldn't believe Kyle chose her to interview Marcy. After her debut with Mudhenge, she'd only done background research for other reporters and an obit for a woman who had lived to be 105. But the editor figured Marcy would more likely trust a reporter of her gender and age. Kyle came up with the idea of interviewing Marcy because police had largely ignored her after an initial interrogation. With the Andersons refusing to talk, Marcy was the best interview subject available to keep the story going.

"I wouldn't even take your notebook into Java Joe's—leave it in the car, and then write down any pertinent facts right after you're done," Kyle had counseled her. "Just go in there and have a nice chitchat, girl-to-girl and see where it goes." Kyle could be a bit off-putting—the "girl-to-girl" remark was a little creepy—but his strategy to pursue Marcy casually on neutral territory made sense to Jenny.

When Jenny arrived at the coffeehouse, a large rectangular space with high ceilings and brick walls adorned with avant-garde, black-and-white photos, she found Marcy at a table in the back near the stage, slathering jelly on a toasted bagel. Except for an elderly couple having breakfast in front, Java Joe's was empty.

"My mom's out running an errand and will be back in about a half hour," Marcy said after Jenny introduced herself and sat down.

For the first few minutes, Jenny let Marcy take the lead in the conversation. Marcy rambled on about being valedictorian and going to Berkeley in August. Jenny was a pleasant change from most people, even strangers, who were overwhelming her with attempts at unwanted emotional support. While Marcy understood most people were just trying to help, their gestures felt intrusive, and at times condescending. The last thing she wanted was to be perceived as the poor, little helpless girl in the wheelchair. Retina Boy was the only person she would open up to about any sadness, fears, or doubts, but without him around, she kept much of her feelings inside.

After ten minutes, Jenny excused herself to get a cup of coffee, and when she returned, Marcy began to talk about her missing friend.

"I just don't get why someone would kidnap him," she said as Jenny opened sugar packets. "I mean, don't the perverts usually go after little kids? I mean, he's eighteen."

"Yeah," Jenny answered, nodding. "So you think he was kidnapped?"

"I guess," said Marcy. "There's just no way he ran off—not the way he loved his band."

"And I understand he was pretty fond of you."

"Well, yeah," said Marcy, looking down at her empty plate, trying unsuccessfully to hide tears.

After wiping her eyes with a napkin, Marcy looked up at Jenny. "Whenever people go missing, the family always believes they'll come back. They never give up until a body is found. I guess it's only natural to never give up hope. But it never seems to end well." Marcy turned her head to make sure the young woman who had just sat at the table behind them wasn't within earshot. "But, I don't know, something doesn't add up with Retina Boy. There's no evidence, no sign of a struggle. And there's no motive... at least that I can think of."

Jenny wished she had her notebook to capture what Marcy was saying—getting the girlfriend's exact take on her boyfriend's disappearance. Nevertheless, she could still paraphrase the points that Marcy was making.

"Seems like the authorities have done everything they can to find him," said Jenny, trying to keep Marcy on the same track. "Is there something you think they should be doing that they aren't?"

Marcy looked toward the front of the coffeehouse where a young woman bouncing a baby in a wrap carrier came through the door. "I guess not," she said. "What do you think? Have you ever covered a disappearance like this before?"

"No, not at all. I'm just an intern. Actually, I'm a senior at Iowa State up in Ames," said Jenny. "I come down once or twice a week and mostly just help out." She shrugged her shoulders and smiled shyly. "So far, I've done only *one* story with a byline. It was on this thing called a mud circle in a farmer's field near Moran. Like a crop circle, but a huge shallow hole. Obviously, there's no corn growing this time of year."

"Yeah, I've heard of crop circles, but not a mud circle. Sounds kinda weird."

"Yeah, it really was bizarre," said Jenny, nodding. "I'm pretty sure the farmer had nothing to do with it. He's just an old guy unsettled by the whole thing. Didn't have much to say. But I got a good photo of it. Ran in the Sunday local section a few weeks ago."

"Cool."

"My editor called it Mudhenge. Now in the newsroom, they call *me* Mudhenge, or sometimes just Muddy," Jenny said, shaking her head.

"But they must like you if they put you on a missing person story," Marcy replied, trying to be encouraging.

"Yeah, they're OK. Listen, before we go, I'd like to get a photo of you." Jenny reached into her jacket for her camera.

Marcy frowned at first, having been caught off guard by the request and reluctant to be photographed in her wheelchair. However, given the numerous yearbook pictures she recently posed for at school, she agreed. At least behind the table, people might not notice the wheelchair.

Jenny moved Marcy's plate and her coffee cup to another table before she took a few shots. Marcy's stoic expression was perfect for the story. With her long blonde curls framing her face, she looked like a lion, a force to be reckoned with.

Marcy looked at her watch. "My mom shouldn't be too much longer."

"OK. Sounds good. One more question, a little more background for the story, if I may," said Jenny as she looked down at her camera, reviewing the shots of Marcy. "Why did you choose to study astronomy? Isn't it a male-dominated field?"

"Yeah, but there are more women going into it. Berkeley has a good program for searching for extraterrestrial life. That's what I'm really interested in. But don't get me wrong—I also like studying about galaxies and black holes, the more standard stuff."

"I should have taken you to see the mud circle, had I known. Could have used your expertise," said Jenny.

"Actually, it sounds kind of cool. Where exactly is it?"

"Not far from Moran."

"Are you going out there again?"

"I wasn't planning on it, but if you want to go, I'd be happy to give Adams a call back," Jenny said. "Problem is, it's on the edge of the property, kind of a long hike, and it is muddy, at least it was."

"That's OK. If he's willing to put me on a tractor, I can get out there. Been on a tractor a couple of times before."

"Yeah, I saw a tractor when I was out there," Jenny said putting on her coat. "OK, I'll give him a call and see if he's up for it."

To Jenny's delight, her story on Marcy ran on the front page of the Tuesday paper, albeit below the fold. The headline read, "Valedictorian Mystified by Blind Boyfriend's Disappearance."

Marcy was pleased to see that her photo was cropped just below her neckline, completely leaving out any sign of the chair.

Chapter 27

Having gained much of his energy back, Retina Boy was eager to leave his cell and get some air and exercise. Ziglo got the subcommittee to agree to let him take a chaperoned excursion through the district before the interviews began.

"He's still in a state of disbelief, and giving him some time in our world is critical to his acclimation and moving forward," Ziglo had argued. "He needs to be completely convinced that he's not on Earth before he can accept anything else we're telling him. He also needs to get a sense of how bad things are on Zooba."

Based on Ziglo's recommendation, the committee agreed to let Retina Boy walk through the nearby commercial sector to Zolobob's store, have a zoofeejee, and then return. His entourage was to include Ziglo, Zeglo, and two guards from the Zohag. No one was concerned he'd try to escape given he had no idea where he was and it had been only a few weeks since he'd left Earth and walked any meaningful distance; he wouldn't have the energy to get far if he tried to flee. In preparation for his outing, Ziglo gave him a warm one-piece garment, like a baggy jumpsuit, and an air pollution mask for his nose and mouth.

As Retina Boy and his entourage exited the incarceration facility, the young Zooban immediately understood why he'd been given the covering for his airways. However, it didn't block out the pollution entirely and his unprotected eyes stung from thick smoke and soot. Though the air was stagnant, he initially imagined being downwind from a wildfire or something burning. He'd smelled wood and leaves burning many times back in Iowa—the smells of fireplaces and backyard parties in the fall—but this was insidious, almost sinister, as if something were burning that shouldn't be.

Arriving in the commercial sector, Retina Boy was overwhelmed by the cacophony of sounds both strange and familiar. Streams of Zooban pedestrians passed by, speaking both rough English, like Ziglo's, and a language he'd never heard before. Many words began with the z sound and sounded to him like swarms of monster insects had invaded. Madonna's "Like a Virgin" blared from an overhead speaker to his left. "Blue Suede Shoes" played in the distance to his right. He heard occasional horns and beeps of varying tones and durations and noticed an unsettling frequency of phlegm-laden coughing and sneezing. The Zee whirring by overhead startled him. And everyone had the same unpleasant body odor that Ziglo had; apparently showering was not a popular habit in this place, wherever it was.

"As I said to you before, Zoobans just adore human culture, especially recent music from the United States and Europe," Ziglo remarked as they moved down the walkway in the sector. "We have several receivers in our cosmic region that intercept Earth's radio signals and route them to processing stations back here. They're broadcast through our public systems and personal devices. That's why you might be hearing familiar music."

"Yeah, we just love it," Zeglo interjected. "We play a lot of Beatles and Rolling Stones back at headquarters. I guess you've probably heard them?"

Retina Boy smiled. "Uh, yeah. Everyone has back on..." As strange as his first few minutes on the streets of Zooba were, Retina Boy couldn't bring himself to complete the sentence to acknowledge he was on an alien planet. "Actually, I have a band, and we play some Beatles covers like 'Let It Be.' I play guitar."

"Whoa, that's great," exclaimed Zeglo. "No one here has figured out how to play music, at least yet. Hey, maybe you could teach us!"

Retina Boy couldn't believe that no one on this alleged planet could play a musical instrument. "Sure, I can help you guys learn, but I need a guitar."

"We've got no guitars here," one of the guards interjected in disappointment.

After a few more minutes in the commercial sector, Retina Boy could no longer deny that he was in a place that was not only unfamiliar, it was outright surreal. What he'd experienced was inexplicable but most unusual was the aura he sensed from anyone who came within a few feet of him. He felt a warm, tingling sensation from Ziglo, Zeglo, the guards, and everyone nearby. It wasn't exactly pleasurable, but it provided a sense of intimacy and comfort—it was similar to what he'd felt from Ziglo when they met. At first, he felt embarrassed by it, as if he was intruding on others' personal spaces. But no one else appeared to mind entering another's personal "energy field." What Retina Boy didn't understand yet was that he was sensing other Zoobans' zill, and that as a Zooban, he had zill as well. He was exactly like the other inhabitants on the planet.

"Our biggest problem is the mining and burning of zool," said Ziglo as they slowed to move through a more congested commercial area. "It's a type of rock that's so plentiful it costs next to nothing and is used by all our factories and anything else that needs energy, including homes and commercial operations. But when it's burned for fuel, it leaves a filthy residue of smoke and particles."

"So that's why everyone's coughing," said Retina Boy. "Even with the mask on, I can tell there's a lot of crud in the atmosphere. My eyes are stinging."

"Yeah, the pollution is so bad it's ruined our water supply and jeopardized a lot of the remaining plant life."

"What about animal life?" asked Retina Boy.

"We've lost seventy-five to eighty percent of our animal population. We have a few animal preservation sites, mostly indoor and heavily secured so we don't lose them all," said Ziglo.

"So what do you eat if you've lost so many animals and plants?"

127

"We clone and grow some animal meat, but it is very costly. Mostly, we eat a few grains we genetically modify to thrive under these less-than-ideal conditions. They're fortified with essentially all the nutrients we need. That's our staple," explained Ziglo as they arrived at Zolobob's store. "That's what the zoofeejee I brought you are made from. Did you like them?"

Before Retina Boy could answer, Zolobob greeted the entourage as they arrived in the dining area of her store. "Welcome," she said, touching Retina Boy's shoulder. The contact with her sent a surge of warmth through his chest and arms. It felt so comforting, he teared up. Not even the most loving, full embrace from Marcy or his parents felt so powerfully soothing. Zolobob's simple touch felt like home.

It was becoming clear to him that these people, these Zoobans as they called themselves, were different, and he experienced an incredibly strong physical connection with them. While he wasn't yet ready to acknowledge they were not human, and that he was actually one of them, he could no longer dismiss the possibility, either.

"I've heard a lot about you. Sit down here, and I'll have some fresh, warm zoofeejee for you in a moment," said Zolobob, excited to meet the young visitor from Earth. As Ziglo had instructed her earlier in the day, she sat Retina Boy and him at one small table, and brought Zeglo and the guards to another. Ziglo wanted to talk with Retina Boy privately.

"How are you doing?" Ziglo asked him after they took stools and sat down. "You must be very tired. You've come a long way."

"Yeah, I'm pretty wiped out, but I'll be OK," said Retina Boy as Zolobob placed a plate with two zoofeejee on the table and walked away. "But where we are, wherever we are, is something else."

"It's completely understandable that you're overwhelmed."

"So you guys eat a lot of zoofeejee?" said Retina Boy as he chewed a corner of one of the warm pastries. "Don't get me wrong, they're pretty tasty."

"They're very popular, and Zolobob makes the best. Most are fortified well enough that you could live off them, and many of the Zoobans who lack wealth do," said Ziglo as he took the other pastry from the plate. "Many of the bigger producers claim theirs' aid in weight loss, but, I don't know, I think they make us a little chunky around the middle."

Zolobob came to the table with a cold bottled beverage that tasted fruity and sweet, almost like Kool Aid. But like the broth that had been brought to Retina Boy's cell, it had a slightly medicinal aftertaste. Nonetheless, it was refreshing to him the Earthling.

Ziglo leaned forward over the table, moving closer to Retina Boy, who continued to sip from the bottle. Ziglo was making sure that what he was about to say wouldn't be heard by anyone nearby. "So as I mentioned before, a committee of the Zog—the Zog is the group who leads and controls our planet—they're going to interview you soon. But I need to prepare you for the interrogation. We need to do all we can to discourage the Zog from the Earth invasion. Will you agree to help me or at least give it a try?"

Retina Boy placed the half-empty bottle down on the table. While he was becoming more and more accepting of the fact that he was in a strange, foreign place populated by people-like beings he had an amazingly close connection with, the phrase "Earth invasion" came across as almost comical, as if it was from the script of an old, low-budget, sci-fi movie. But at the same time, he felt like he had no choice but to play along—for his own safety and well-being. Perhaps if he met this group called the Zog, he would learn more about his predicament and, most important, a way out of it. What else could he do?

"OK," answered Retina Boy. "I'll help you, but only under one condition."

Chapter 28

"Well, I scanned and emailed all the signed forms for Berkeley," said Marcy after finishing a bite of a grilled Tofurky, lettuce, and tomato sandwich. "All that's left is getting me a place to live, and they said they're working on it. All I know is they want to keep me on campus."

"Good. I know its hard right now thinking about school in August," said her mom, walking from the kitchen into the dining room with a small plate of chocolate chip cookies as her father went in the opposite direction.

"Would it be too much to ask to get some real bacon for me next time?" he said before opening the door of the refrigerator.

Marcy rolled her eyes as her mom returned and smiled back forgivingly.

"Oh, you got something from Amazon today. I put it on your bed," her mom said while putting a cookie on Marcy's plate.

"Better save at least one of those cookies for me," her dad yelled from the kitchen.

"OK. Thanks, mom," said Marcy, struggling to recall what she had ordered. Most of her purchases were downloads of music and e-books. Maybe someone had sent her a gift. If it was for Valentine's Day, it was a few days late. The well-wishing emails and cards had stopped coming for the most part. For a few weeks, the disappearance of her boyfriend had been the talk of Des Moines, but with no new evidence or leads, the chatter and media coverage had died down considerably. Even Marcy herself was trying to focus on the summer ahead.

The box from Amazon was small and rectangular, like a box that business cards would come in. She tore through the packing tape with one of her house keys. When she pulled the lid up and removed the brown paper packing material, she found a small thin black disk, not quite the diameter of a dime, in a clear plastic sleeve. At the bottom of the box was a printed note that read:

> This is private for Marcy only. Sit near a window in
> a quiet, unoccupied room. Squeeze front and back of
> unwrapped disk between thumb and index finger. After
> 45 to 60 seconds, the disk should beep three times. If it
> doesn't beep, move to a different window. After third beep,
> hold disk on edges very close to ear. Listen carefully for the
> fun celebratory message. The message will not repeat.

Marcy was captivated as she examined the disk still in its sleeve. Who would have sent her such a cool piece of technology? She'd never seen anything like it before. What a great idea for a gift. Hopefully, it wasn't a prank. She slid across her bed to get near the window facing south, overlooking the backyard. Then she pulled on a cord to open the blinds. It was a crisp, clear winter evening, about twenty minutes after sunset—the horizon glowing pink and orange behind the tall, leafless trees that lined the edge of the backyard.

Marcy removed the disk from the sleeve and held it a few inches from the window as she squeezed it. In her excitement, she realized she'd forgotten to look at her watch to determine when a minute had passed.

After what seemed like an eternity, she muttered, "Shit," as she examined the disk. She shook it and then held it up to the window again. If it didn't play the message on the next attempt, she'd go into her dad's office and try the window facing west.

But after about forty seconds, the three beeps came, each a few seconds apart. Marcy held the tiny device up to her ear by the edges as instructed. About ten seconds after the third beep, she was shocked to hear a familiar voice speaking deliberately and calmly:

> Marcy. Hi. It's Retina Boy. First, I'm fine. Please don't be
> worried. I'm not in any danger, but I can't tell you where
> I am. I've been told it's very far away, but I'm not certain.
> Marcy. This is not a joke or a hoax. This is really me. Really!

Then, silence for a few seconds.

> There should be a clue to what happened to me just south of
> Moran, Iowa, at the following GPS coordinates: forty-one
> degrees, seventy-six minutes north, and ninety-three degrees,
> ninety-two minutes west. I repeat: forty-one, seventy-six,
> and ninety-three, ninety-two. One more time: forty-one,
> seventy-six, and ninety-three, ninety-two. This isn't exact,
> but it should be close. That's what someone told me.

Retina Boy coughed and cleared his throat.

> You can't tell anyone about this message. If you do, it will
> jeopardize my safety. I miss you so much, Marcy. I love you
> so much. Please don't worry. I'm fine. Really, I am. Goodbye,
> Marcy. I love you. Again, don't tell anyone about this. Not
> even anyone in the band. Goodbye. I miss you so much.

Exasperated, Marcy quickly pulled herself over to the nightstand on the other side of the bed, opened the top drawer, and pulled out an envelope and a pen. She wrote down the four numbers as the voice of Retina Boy had instructed: forty-one, seventy-six, ninety-three, ninety-two. She felt her heart pounding in her chest. She could barely catch her breath. She remembered what he said about Moran, Iowa—the clue to his whereabouts was near there. Someone else had recently mentioned Moran. It was Jenny, the reporter who covered the mud circle. Jenny said the mud circle was near Moran. "No way," Marcy whispered to herself. "No way."

Hearing Retina Boy's voice was an incredible relief for her. The recording really sounded like him. It had to be him. She sat up in her bed and stared out the window.

After a couple of minutes, she put the disk back in the box and saw that she had missed some of its contents: two pieces of very thin turquoise rope, each about a half inch long—the ends from his friendship bracelet.

Unable to logically process and accept for fact everything that had just happened, she concluded that Retina Boy was alive. Somewhere. He had to be. She was overjoyed, but at the same time afraid something was terribly wrong.

Chapter 29

Retina Boy didn't expect the conference room to be so cramped and stuffy. The smell of it reminded him of the boys' gym lockers at his high school back in Iowa. It was as if his classmates had left their sweaty gym clothes stuffed in lockers for days, which they often did. As unpleasant as the odor was, its familiarity was oddly comforting.

His nervous anticipation of the questioning also reminded him of the show-and-tell episode in elementary school, when he embarrassingly demonstrated his cane and talked about his blindness in front of the whole class. He had felt like a freak show. And here he was again, in God knows where, on display.

The eleven committee members and Ziglo sat at a U-shaped table with Retina Boy sitting in a chair a few feet beyond the open end. About twenty other spectators sat behind him.

The committee members were formidably large males—tall and large bellied—with long, bushy hair and beards. Many were graying with balding crowns. They were clad in robes that were either gray or beige and pocked with food stains and small tears.

The proceedings began with little formality. Zeglo introduced Zebnee, a senior member of the Zog known for his eloquence and alleged expertise in Zooban anatomy and physiology. He would lead the proceedings.

"First, I want to say welcome home, Zin," said Zebnee in a low gravelly voice. Zebnee had stubbornly refused to wear an air pollution mask for many years to convey to the public that Zooba wasn't an unhealthy place to live. Ultimately, lung and esophageal damage convinced him to protect his respiratory system. "Without realizing, you bravely spent many years of your young life on an alien planet as a service to Zooba. You are a hero to all of us."

Retina Boy didn't respond. The last thing he expected was to be called a hero. He felt more like a captive. Also, being referred to as Zin was unsettling. It was as if they were mistaking him for someone else.

Zebnee continued. "Using a tiny transmitter implanted in your buttocks, we monitored your health throughout your time on Earth. I am pleased to say you remained remarkably well. The Earth's air and water appear to suit you, and your immune system did a surprisingly good job fighting off pathogens. Also, your consumption of plant and animal life enabled you to thrive."

"Uh, I just want to say," Retina Boy nervously interjected. "I don't eat animals anymore. I mean, I did for a long time. But I don't now. Only plants. Sometimes eggs and milk." His remark elicited unintelligible chatter from the back of the room. One of the committee members whispered something to Zebnee.

"OK, we'll make a note of that dietary information," Zebnee replied. He said a few words in Zooban back to the committee member, and then continued with the questioning. "Yes, as I said, our data indicate that you were healthy on Earth, but we were wondering if you experienced any illnesses that Earthling medical experts thought were unusual."

"No, not really. Except that I'm blind. They did genetic research to try to figure out the cause of my blindness. They're still doing it—looking for the genes. Dr. Strong at the University of Iowa is my doctor and the lead scientist."

Zebnee forced a cough to clear his lungs. "So they never figured out the cause?" he asked.

"No, they're really frustrated that they can't."

Someone in the back of the room laughed.

"OK, that's all the questions I have for now," said Zebnee. "Zedlar, please proceed with your inquiry."

While preparing Retina Boy for the interview, Ziglo had mentioned that Zedlar was the committee member most knowledgeable about the evolving invasion and occupation plan, and had a strong influence on the strategy and tactics. "He may have many questions, or he may choose to ask or reveal very little," Ziglo had said. "While we need to dissuade him from launching the invasion, we at least have to try to convince him that a hostile approach will fail. But don't be too antagonistic. You're Zooban, and you need to act like you're on their side."

Ziglo was pleased that Zedlar had decided to actively take part in the interrogation because it would give Retina Boy an opportunity to potentially influence decisions about the invasion.

"Thank you for your service to Zooba," said Zedlar. "You are to be commended." He spoke so slowly and deliberately, it seemed to take several minutes for him to get just those few words out. He was the eldest member of the committee and had the best command of English; he sounded more like an American than any other Zooban that Retina Boy had heard.

Zedlar didn't waste any time cutting to the chase. "How do you think Earthlings will react to the arrival of Zoobans? Do you think they will welcome us if we try to come in peace?" he asked matter-of-factly. The question caught Retina Boy off guard. The others in the room were also surprised that Zedlar had been so direct so quickly. They held their breath as they waited for Retina Boy to answer.

"Well, I think they'll freak out," said Retina Boy as he sat up taller in his chair. "I mean, we've never met anyone from another planet. You will shock everyone."

"So do you think it would be better to launch the invasion without trying to establish an amicable relationship first?"

Retina Boy was surprised again by the weighty question. What neither he nor Ziglo knew was that this issue was the subject of contentious internal debate within the Zog. Some members of the invasion committee had hoped to build rapport with key Earthlings in different countries to learn the planet's infrastructure. If they could build alliances, perhaps some of the Earthlings would actually support Zooba's takeover. But other members felt that an invasion needed to be swift and decisive to be successful; there could be no middle ground with the Earthlings.

"How do you plan to invade? Will you use military force?" replied Retina Boy, following a course for the discussion that Ziglo had counseled him to take. They needed as much information about a hostile invasion as they could gather to build a case against it.

Zedlar snorted loudly while adjusting himself in his chair. "Right now, we are considering a biological assault," he said. "We also need to disable their power grids and communications infrastructure."

The remark elicited grumbling and whispering from the back of the room.

Ziglo saw the moment as an excellent opportunity to dampen the Zog's enthusiasm for hostility and violence. "Zin, do you think the Earthlings will be quick to strike back or will they recognize the futility in doing so?" he interjected quickly before anyone else had a chance to speak.

"I think the biggest problem is that you are all blind, and you won't be able to react well to everything that's going on," said Retina Boy. "I got around OK in my neighborhood, near my school, and places that I knew. But it was tough when I traveled to other cities. Cars and bikes could be big trouble—they move so fast."

This was not the answer Ziglo wanted, but Retina Boy had made an important point that needed to be made: blindness was a critical weakness for Zoobans.

Retina Boy continued after no one responded to his answer, remembering what Ziglo had counseled him to say about the potential response to a hostile invasion. "As you know, there are nuclear weapons deployed all over Earth, and if just one or two gets launched, that could be horrible for the environment. Then Earth would be no better off than Zooba—maybe worse—with all the radiation."

"Also, we don't know how the biological weapon will impact Earth's plants or animals," Ziglo noted.

More buzzing and grumbling came from the back of the room.

Zebnee neither wanted nor expected the interrogation to focus directly on the invasion or its consequences. That subject matter was for a different committee, the group planning the invasion. Rather, he hoped his committee's questions would reveal details of Zin's health and the living conditions and social habits and mores of humans—information that might help shape the high-level strategies for occupation. He had invited Zedlar as a courtesy, to keep him in the loop politically. So Zebnee abruptly concluded the session, indicating only that he wanted to talk with the committee members privately and they would reconvene soon.

Ziglo joined the guards walking Retina Boy back to his cell. "Things got a little off track," he whispered to Retina Boy as they walked a few steps ahead of the security entourage. "But I think you helped open the door to our plan. You raised some uncertainty and doubt. That was good."

As they arrived at the cell, Ziglo said, "Look, I'm not going to come in right now. You just get some rest. Oh, and your friend Marcy got the package. We received confirmation that she activated the audio disk. Hopefully, she'll keep quiet about it for now. Regardless, I doubt anyone on Earth is going to consider that you were abducted by aliens."

Exhausted from the proceedings, Retina Boy immediately plopped down on his bed. He was glad to be done with the first round of questioning, but most of all, he was relieved to hear that Marcy knew he was OK. Of course, she, his family, and the band would be worried sick about his disappearance. Hopefully, Marcy would get some comfort from his message, even if it left several questions unanswered, most notably, his whereabouts.

Though he still felt skeptical that he was on another planet, his disbelief had diminished considerably. The interrogation, the walk through Zooba's commercial sector, his interactions with Ziglo and other Zoobans—they had all become his reality, which was too elaborate and conspicuous to deny. No one had come by to give him medication. There was no therapist or psychiatrist trying to counsel him about bizarre illusions or hallucinations. He hadn't awoken from some crazy dream. And except for a few random pop tunes he'd heard during his excursion, virtually nothing in his new reality was earthly.

Chapter 30

With her morning sickness and zing addiction withdrawals past, along with the overwhelming fear that her pregnancy would have catastrophic consequences for her and her Earth-boy lover, Zellie clapped her hands and twirled around Doug's cell, singing over and over, "Let the sunshine, let the sunshine in, the sun shine in." Her lack of inhibition for the moment concerned Doug—perhaps the guards would reprimand them for her rowdiness—but security had ignored them for so long, including their loud moans and groans from sex, that he didn't try to stop her.

Zellie as she danced and sang looked astonishingly beautiful to Doug—her baby bump beginning to show, her wiggling hips, and her long red hair flowing as she moved around the room. He couldn't believe how happy she was, nor had he ever known what a powerful singing voice she had. She sounded as good as the females he'd listened to on the music broadcasts from Earth. Zellie had never been more alluring to him.

As he slowly emerged from deep sleep, Retina Boy thought he was back home in his basement, with his mom listening to her favorite album, *The 5th Dimension's Greatest Hits*. But the female voice, while bold and soulful, was not familiar. And why was *he* listening to that song? Then he realized the music was coming from the other side of the wall of his cell. He was still in Zooba.

Retina Boy presumed it was Zellie. Ziglo had told him about her, the young Zooban woman carrying Doug-the-Earthling's child, who if it could see had the potential to halt or delay the invasion by providing a distraction from it.

Zellie's a cappella performance got Retina Boy wondering what Rhodopsin was up to without him. Were they practicing? Were they playing gigs? He also missed his Martin and his Stratocaster guitars. Hopefully, he hadn't forgotten how to play or lost too much finger strength and agility. While he wasn't sure how long he'd been away—it had to have been several weeks—he'd never gone for so long without practicing.

When Ziglo arrived a short time later to discuss a plan for the next interrogation session, he asked Retina Boy if he'd heard Zellie's singing. "Yeah, it actually woke me up. But her voice is so beautiful, better than back home. I was impressed."

"Well, she's the talk of the Zohag at the moment. Apparently, all the guards heard her. They were practically swooning," said Ziglo. "You have to understand, Zoobans normally don't sing. They love to listen to music, but they have no aptitude for it. But they're obsessed with it. They're practically hypnotized when they really listen."

"So no one on Zooba plays music?"

"No. Zellie's little performance is the first time I've heard of any Zooban doing anything musical."

"You know, I play guitar," said Retina Boy. "I even have a band back home. We're pretty good. We get a lot of cool gigs."

"Yes, I think you mentioned that before."

"Yeah. But who knows what they're doing without me around. Hopefully, they're still practicing. A couple of the guys can be real slackers."

Ziglo, who'd been sitting next to Retina Boy on his bed, stood up and slowly walked to the other side of the room, turned around, and then came back to the foot of the bed. "Do your friends like to travel?" he asked.

"Well, yeah, I guess. Sammy was talking about us going to Florida on spring break."

Ziglo didn't respond. He just stood silent, in deep thought. He walked across the cell again and let out a laugh when he reached the other side.

Surely the committee would think he was completely mad with the audacious plan that had just come to him. However, he also knew the committee realized that an invasion was fraught with risk and the potential for devastating, long-term outcomes.

It didn't take long for Retina Boy to figure out what Ziglo meant by his comment, "Do your friends like to travel?" but the large Zooban's overall plan, as he was about to explain it, was never something that Retina Boy would have ever imagined. As if already being on a planet called Zooba and being Zooban himself wasn't crazy enough.

Chapter 31

Not only had the committee tasked with interrogating Retina Boy been thrown somewhat off course during its first session, the committee planning the invasion was at loggerheads after its first two meetings. It was charged with determining invasion timing, strategy, and tactics, but a growing faction of its members was beginning to question the feasibility of a complete Earth takeover. With Earth's diversity—its hundreds of countries governed by numerous political systems—the committee had reported there were "too many unknowns and variables." Also, as Retina Boy and Ziglo had testified, the risk of a large-scale environmental disaster from retaliation was significant. However, the pro-invasion members argued that Zooba was doomed without a quick and decisive occupation.

For Ziglo, the Zog's inability to formulate an invasion plan provided him with a window of opportunity to thwart it. He told Zeglo that he had "new data" that might help break the stalemate. "But you have to let me present it to both the interrogation and invasion committees at the same time," he had said. "And no observers. We can't let this information go public—yet. But we need Zin there."

Zeglo was reluctant to request that the two committees convene together given that each was having its difficulties functioning independently. He was also unhappy that Ziglo wouldn't tell him what the "new data" was. But with his pal's urging, he agreed to approach Zedlar with the idea, and to his surprise, Zedlar commended him for it, namely because there was no other path for the committees to move forward. He welcomed the report of new information; it might help break the stalemates.

Retina Boy sat in the middle of the interrogation room while members of the committees arrived. He was less worried about his actual testimony than what Marcy would think of the plan, if and when she arrived in Zooba. He and Ziglo agreed that asking her and a few friends to travel to another planet would never work. They'd likely think it was a hoax, and in the event they did believe they were going to an alien land, there's no way they'd stay quiet about it. Friends and family would be in disbelief but, regardless, would never let them attempt to leave.

"Be vague. Just tell your girlfriend it's going to be a journey or some type of meeting and that she'll better understand once she gets to the destination and reunites with you," Ziglo had said. "But ensure her it will be safe. She has to believe you."

"I guess I shouldn't tell her about the really bad space lag," Retina Boy had joked, recalling how long it took him to recover from the journey.

However, what Retina Boy dreaded most was lying to Marcy and potentially delaying her Berkeley plans. The last thing he ever wanted was to quash her dream of becoming a world-class astronomer. But, then again, why go to school to study extraterrestrial life when she could actually commune with it?

Ziglo, Zeglo, and Retina Boy stood at the front of the conference room next to Zedlar and Zebnee who were seated. Other members of the committees sat on stools throughout the room, though most of the invasion committee members were sitting in back. After the last member hurried into the room and the door slid shut, Zeglo began the proceedings. "Thanks to both committees for agreeing to meet. We are convening because our committee's consultant, Ziglo, has new important data to share that he believes will have a major impact on our invasion and occupation plans. Ziglo, please begin."

Ziglo and Retina Boy walked to the middle of the room. Ziglo was anxious about giving testimony in front of so many high-ranking officials. He was never politically active nor had he had much public speaking experience when he worked as a criminal-processing officer. Furthermore, he was lacking confidence about his plan. Though it sounded good when he talked about it, there were many ways it could fail. First and foremost, he worried that Retina Boy's Earthling pals wouldn't follow their friend's instructions to meet for some ambiguous gathering in a remote field. And, if they did make it to Zooba, how would they react to being asked to live in a toxic wasteland with consumption-addicted aliens? However, he couldn't come up with a better alternative strategy. It was his best shot.

"Thank you Zeglo and committee members. I recently became aware of a development that could have a major impact on our species and life here on Zooba," said Ziglo in disbelief that he was uttering such a dramatic statement to the Zog. "As you know, we've been holding the Earthling, the male who goes by the name of Doug, in captivity in the Zohag. And we've allowed visitors, namely a female, who was formerly Doug's caretaker. Her name is Zellie. Well, Doug has impregnated Zellie."

Ziglo paused. Except for some wheezing from one of the committee members, the room was silent.

"Thus far, the progeny is healthy and doing well. It's female," said Ziglo as coughing came from the front and back of the room. "I had Zellie evaluated by a medical team in my district."

"Why are you telling us this now? Why did you wait?" yelled one of the invasion committee members.

"We only recently learned that the pregnancy was viable," Ziglo answered calmly. "I had no intention of withholding the information."

"And why did you take it upon yourself to help this female get medical care?" asked the same member, dismayed by what he perceived as a lack of protocol and transparency. "Who gave you authorization to help the Earthling?"

To Ziglo's surprise, Zeglo spoke up in his defense. "Ziglo and I originally arrested and processed the Earthling when he was caught

147

shoplifting," he said. "When Ziglo retired, he visited Doug. Zellie and Ziglo were Doug's only visitors."

"Yes, I got permission... uh... authorization from the Zohag to visit Doug," added Ziglo. "The visits were just out of benevolence. And I got to know Zellie in the process."

"So now we have this cross-species child?" interjected someone from the interrogation group. "A chimera!"

"That's correct," answered Ziglo. "But remember: Zoobans and humans differ by only a few genes; we are very similar. And this new child could have some important implications for our future." Ziglo paused to make sure there were no more questions or concerns. He was about to deliver the most critical part of his testimony. He didn't want any interruptions or distractions as he moved forward.

"I had the child genetically screened, and she has three of the four human gene variations for eyesight," he explained. "I recognize that we don't know if that is enough for the child to see with her eyes, but even if she doesn't, I expect that our scientists will learn a lot from her, especially if the child is healthy."

"So do you suggest we have the Earthling Doug impregnate more Zooban females?" asked Zebnee.

"Well, possibly, but I think it would be best to bring more Earthlings to Zooba—we need the genetic diversity. Also, we need to figure out how many of the genes it will take to give Zoobans eyesight. Zellie's child will be a good start toward determining that number."

A loud groan came from someone on the invasion committee. Then another member of the invasion contingent laughed facetiously.

But, Zebnee was intrigued by the proposed genetic experiment. "So how do you suggest we bring additional Earthlings here? Abduct them?" he asked.

"Zin believes he can convince them to come here under their own volition. Well, sort of," said Ziglo, tapping once on Retina Boy's shoulder.

"Uh, yeah," said Retina Boy, hesitantly. "Uh, I think some of my friends will be excited to travel here, to Zooba, to learn about your planet. I have one friend, actually, my girlfriend, who is very interested in extraterrestrial life—life on other planets like Zooba."

Before anyone else could interrupt or comment, Ziglo continued elaborating on the plan and the impetus for it. "I believe by bringing more Earthlings here and raising our citizen's excitement about the prospects of eyesight, we can begin to draw Zooba's attention away from consumption," he said in a raised voice. He was feeling more confident. "It wouldn't be just about vision, we could learn more about Earth's culture and music, which we're obviously very excited and passionate about."

"But do you *really* think that's enough to diminish our insatiable appetite for material possessions?" asked Zebnee. "I can't believe that a visit from a few Earthlings will be enough."

"But an Earth invasion isn't the answer, either," replied an unidentified detractor from the invasion committee. "If we take over Earth, we'll end up destroying its environment as well."

Several loud groans came from around the room.

"Please, comrades!" shouted Zebnee. "Please. Let's show respect."

By clearing his throat loudly and deliberately, Zedlar brought silence to the conference room. "There are some important points being made," he said. "While I am by no means trying to completely dismiss the idea of an invasion, I agree that it is a potentially hazardous course of action. I am not sure it is the long-term solution to our environmental dilemma."

"I have one more important element of our proposed plan," Ziglo said immediately after Zedlar finished. "I suggest we eventually send a small contingent of Zoobans to Earth. There are many things we can learn better by being there, including strategies for conservation."

"So you're suggesting an exchange of sorts," said Zebnee.

"Yes. Exactly."

Quiet pervaded the meeting room. Ziglo was relieved to hear no groaning, laughing, or detracting comments. Maybe his plan was beginning to gain some traction, or at least the opposition to it was quelled by Zebnee's and Zedlar's openness to hearing about it.

"Of course, if this proposed swap of Earthlings and Zoobans doesn't work, we could still invade," Zedlar commented. "We need to establish some parameters with time being a critical one."

"Good point," added Zebnee.

No more remarks came from the committees.

Sensing the discussion was coming to an end with his friend's plan having garnered some support, Zeglo said, "OK, I suggest a short recess before the two committees convene privately."

"Just one more item before we conclude," said Ziglo. "Zin, tell them about your idea for music."

Retina Boy stood up and took a few steps backward, moving toward his right, so he could talk more clearly to the committees. For the first time during his testimonies, he felt as if he was about to give a performance, though without his guitar strapped on, he felt awkward.

"If we can get my band and our instruments here, we can hold a live concert," he said. "It could be Zooba's first-ever live music performance, and I think it would be really cool. And if you want, we can also teach you guys how to play."

"Can you play some Jimi Hendrix?" Zeglo asked. "Do you know that musician?"

Retina Boy grinned. "You bet, dude," he said, "You bet."

Chapter 32

Marcy usually devoured vegan pizza when someone remembered to special order it for her from University Zahs. Even though the pie was made of only crust, tomato sauce, mushrooms, green peppers, and black olives, she considered it a special treat. People were often in disbelief that she enjoyed it so much and made comments like, "Really, you can eat that without cheese?" or "Isn't that just bread and tomato sauce? Doesn't sound very good."

But none of the dozen guests in the Pullman's dining room noticed her disinterest in the meat-free pizza on that Thursday evening in March. They were celebrating Danny's good news: the gene therapy for his retinitis pigmentosa appeared to be working. Dr. Strong determined that his visual field had expanded in his treated eye while it had contracted slightly in his untreated eye. The results were even better than expected. Dr. Strong had thought that at best, the therapy would halt or slow Danny's vision loss. Restored vision, a wider visual field, was a bonus.

"Yeah, they're going to schedule me to have my other eye treated pretty soon," Danny said as everyone around the table listened intently and ate. He himself hadn't noticed any difference in his vision since the treatment, but the positive test results were good enough for him. "Dr. Strong is pretty pumped about the whole thing. He says I need to be cautious about getting too excited. They want to see how well it works over several years. But it's obvious he's pretty happy."

"Well, even if the therapy can just help you keep the vision you have, that would be huge," said Marc Pullman, holding a half-eaten slice above his plate. Everyone around the table, which included Justin, Jake, Sammy, and a few other friends from school, nodded in agreement as they ate.

However, all Marcy could think about was the second disk she'd received. She'd felt discombobulated by the first disk that had come in the mail a couple of weeks earlier with Retina Boy's audio message. On one hand, she was excited to receive evidence that he was apparently OK. However, the disks themselves, the way they had been delivered, were so strange and mysterious. She was constantly preoccupied, wondering where he was, why he was gone, and who might be behind the abduction, if that's what actually had occurred. She found it difficult to make sense of what was happening. There were moments of hope—the knowledge that at least he was alive, probably. It was better than having absolutely no clues at all.

The coordinates he'd given her that pointed to Mudhenge had been particularly confounding. She thought perhaps that someone was playing some kind of twisted game with her. The idea that he'd been abducted by aliens did cross her mind, but she ultimately dismissed it as absurd. She couldn't allow herself to believe such nonsense.

But now there was the second disk with an audio message in which he implored her to get all the members of the band, or as many as she could, out to the mud circle on the evening of the spring equinox, March 20. "Tell them it's a celebration of spring or maybe a vigil for me. Whatever reason you want," he had said on the recording, trying to be encouraging. "You need to be out there around seven thirty or eight in the evening. Hopefully, the weather won't be too bad. If you can build a fire, that would help a lot. And it would keep you guys warm."

Fortunately, Jenny gladly helped organize the gathering at Mudhenge. She got Adams to agree to let Marcy and her friends build a bonfire on his land in a tribute to their missing blind friend. And he was happy to pull them with a tractor out to the mud circle, now frozen solid. "I've got firewood for you, if you want it," Adams had said to her on the phone. "Winter hasn't been too bad, so I have plenty extra."

Marcy felt conflicted about asking Jenny to join them. It only seemed right to include her since she'd gotten the farmer to let them use the land. Also, Jenny had a car—she could drive everyone and avoid getting any parents involved. But in his message, Retina Boy had only asked for Marcy and the band members. She wondered if an uninvited participant might cause problems.

In his second message, Retina Boy instructed Marcy to send an email confirming the evening gathering at the specified coordinates on March 20 to zig.x97@zooba.net. In her reply, she answered, "Yes, plus one additional guest." She never received a reply, so she decided to invite Jenny, who was happy to come along. "But no story in the newspaper this time, please," Marcy told her on the phone. "I don't want anyone else to know about the vigil."

All the members of Rhodopsin except Sammy agreed to participate in the vigil. They thought it was a cool and fitting thing to do, as long as the weather held out. Sammy was instead going on his previously planned spring break road trip with three other seniors to Florida.

Though they had cancelled all their gigs, Rhodopsin managed to hold a practice every week or two since Retina Boy's disappearance. However, they floundered without a lead guitarist. Justin tried to lead with keyboards, and while he was a skilled player, he lacked the edgy and powerful sound that Retina Boy delivered with his Stratocaster. As Jake had said after a few practices, "We're beginning to sound like soft rock. It's kind of bumming me out."

The boys were also beginning to think about college the next year. Justin was staying in town to attend Drake, while Jake, Danny, and Retina Boy had been accepted at the University of Iowa. Sammy was also trying to get into the University of Iowa, but as a C+ student, he was put on a waiting list. While the boys were notably upset by the disappearance of their friend, especially for the first few weeks after he went missing, they were also moving on with their lives. But the vigil was the first time as a band that they would formally commemorate Retina Boy, and with the publicity about him diminishing, it felt to them like the right time to do it.

Except for Marcy and the band, everyone else who came to the impromptu pizza party left after about an hour, and Danny's parents went into their living room to watch *Parks and Recreation*, their favorite TV program. "See ya, kids," said Marc as he and Meg stood up to leave. "My hero Ron Swanson calls."

Sammy opened the lids of each of the pizza boxes, letting out a sigh of disappointment after realizing that all were empty except the one with the vegan slices. He picked one up reluctantly.

"I still can't believe Retina Boy's gone," Danny said, shaking his head and picking up some crumbs from the table and dropping them into an empty pizza box.

Though the conversation had stopped, and the moment warranted someone breaking the silence, no one expected Danny to bring up their missing pal. The dining room went quiet again, except for the din of the nearby television.

Then Justin said, "Are we supposed to bring anything to the vigil?" as Danny picked up the empty pizza boxes. "Would it be weird to bring food?"

"What about s'mores?" Jake blurted out, looking toward Marcy for approval.

"I guess so," Marcy replied shrugging her shoulders. "I can ask my mom or dad to pick up the stuff we need to make them from Campbell's. We have barbecue skewers, too, for toasting the marshmallows. I'll make sure my mom gets the vegan brand."

Marcy couldn't believe she'd just agreed to snacks for a gathering that could lead to the end of them all. Who knew what might happen out there in the middle of the farmer's field? For all she knew, they would be chopped up into small pieces and then cooked in the bonfire, their ashes spread out all over the field like fertilizer! Or maybe they'd be abducted and sold as sex slaves to some obscure criminal group in Southeast Asia.

She trusted Retina Boy more than anyone. Sure, he was sometimes distracted by his music and Rhodopsin, especially when they had an upcoming gig, but he had never lied to her. And he had sounded so sincere and sure of himself on the recordings. She didn't believe he was being coerced or reading a prepared statement. Initially, Marcy's biggest hope in going to Mudhenge was being reunited with him. But now, with the vigil only two days away, she worried more about her own safety and the well-being of everyone else she'd asked to go along. While Marcy prided herself in her own honesty and integrity, she understood that she had, in effect, lied about the reason for the vigil. However, at this point she felt there was no turning back.

Chapter 33

After urging from his wife, Fred Adams scheduled an appointment with a neurologist in early April. He could no longer deny he was having significant memory issues. He'd recently searched for a missing toolbox for three days only to discover he left it in the barn, where he'd been repairing a door hinge, a project he'd forgotten to finish.

But on this first day of spring, he was happy to be taking Jenny, Marcy, and her pals out into his field, his old tractor puttering along slowly as it pulled a wooden cart with the five young passengers. It was a clear, windless evening, about a half hour before sunset. Though the temperature had reached fifty that afternoon, the ground remained frozen solid from an extended seasonal cold spell. Adams usually didn't have much reason to venture far onto his property at dusk in winter, but on this evening, as he gazed out west he admired the bright orange, peach, and yellow horizon over his quiescent fields. Regardless of whatever was happening inside his brain, he, at the moment, felt proud to have worked his land for more than four decades.

With the vigil about to come to fruition, Marcy had a difficult time believing that anything good was going to come of it. She felt more certain she'd responded to a hoax. So many bad things could happen out in the middle of nowhere. Hopefully, there were no pranksters watching or recording them. How embarrassing it would be. Who could be so sick as to pull a stunt like this? Marcy also wasn't pleased with having to use crutches instead of her wheelchair due to the rugged terrain. She was clumsy with them, and because her arms fatigued quickly, she sometimes fell if she had to walk more than a few feet.

"I hope you can finish up by ten, ten thirty. That's about our bedtime," said Adams as he helped the boys unload firewood.

"I'm sure we will," answered Marcy as she tested the solidness of the ground with her right crutch. "I don't see us lasting out here more than two hours. I've got your number in my cell phone."

After choosing a spot just a few yards from the edge of Mudhenge, Danny and Justin began to build a pyramid with the large haul of newspapers, sticks, and logs that Adams provided. Jake brought along a container of charcoal lighter to ensure they wouldn't have any problem getting the bonfire started.

Jake was fascinated with the vast, shallow depression in the earth as he slowly walked around its perimeter. He considered going inside the oval but felt it would be like a trespass of sacred ground. Whatever had made this recess in the earth warranted respect. After he got about fifty yards from the group, he shouted, "Can you believe this thing? Who the hell did it?" Everyone looked up at him, but no one responded.

Jenny and Marcy sat next to each other on nylon foldout chairs as they watched the fire being built. "I think this was a nice idea... for you and his friends to pay tribute... or just take time to... say how much you miss him," said Jenny, choosing her words carefully.

"Yeah, I don't know," said Marcy as she watched Danny squirt lighter fluid on the large pile of sticks and logs. "It's all been *so weird*." Marcy was tempted to tell Jenny about the disks, or at least the fact that she'd gotten what appeared to be messages from Retina Boy. But while she trusted her, Marcy didn't know if Jenny would be ethically obliged to report the disclosure of evidence to the authorities. So she didn't say anything.

Danny pulled out a box of blue tip matches, lit one, and threw it on the pile. He smiled back at Justin as it went up in a whoosh of flames.

"Well, that was easy," said Justin, folding out a chair.

It was dusk as the five teenagers held out long skewers tipped with marshmallows near the fire. The sky above had darkened to deep indigo. Marcy gazed out at what she surmised were Jupiter and Sirius, the Dog Star, hovering over the southern horizon. She imagined staying up all night next to the mud circle to track the stars and constellations as they moved across the sky.

She also realized how much Retina Boy would have enjoyed the outing—communing with nature on a crisp winter night and hanging out with friends. Her eyes began to tear a little, but no one noticed because the flickering flames in the darkness made everyone's eyes look glassy. She felt relief in her sadness. Without distractions, she was able to let herself grieve her loss. It was a rare moment that Marcy was able to let go, though she was careful not to break down sobbing in front of the others.

After looking at her browned marshmallow, she glanced down at her watch. The green glowing numbers displayed "8:21." Other than the popping and crackling coming from the fire, it was remarkably quiet. Only a hint of the day's sunlight, a deep-blue glow, remained in the southwestern sky.

A few minutes later, Justin heard a whirring sound overhead and looked up. Retina Boy had always said that Rhodopsin's keyboard player had the best hearing of anyone in the band. Justin picked up hums, buzzes, and missed notes that no one else noticed.

Soon, everyone else heard the noise as well. Looking up, they saw a large dark oval silhouette in the sky. It appeared to be descending toward them.

They would never remember what happened next.

Chapter 34

Unlike his initial time on Zooba when he had trouble staying awake, Retina Boy now found sleep hard to come by. For one thing, the Zog allowed Zellie to visit Doug on a regular basis—she practically lived with him—and they were a rambunctious couple, often shouting and laughing, especially when they discussed plans for their forthcoming child.

On this particular morning, Retina Boy awoke to an impassioned argument about names. "Does she have to have a *z* name like everyone else around here?" Doug whined. "What about Aretha? I love that name! And you're always singing that 'natural woman' song."

Zellie responded loudly but in a slow cadence, trying to be assertive while not letting the debate spiral out of control. "Look, I don't want her to stand out. I want her to be just like the rest of the kids," she said.

"Really?" Doug exclaimed. "Really? The kid's going to be half-human, half-Zooban. How will she *not* stand out?"

Retina Boy thought Doug made a good point. No one knew exactly what this child would be like. Ziglo had said that thus far she appeared to be developing normally. She had all her fingers and toes, and all her vital signs were good. Ziglo had also noted that the researchers probably knew her genetic makeup, if she had some or all of the genes for vision, and he was trying to ascertain that information. But in many respects, the hybrid child was still a mystery.

Retina Boy could hear Zellie talking more but not loud enough to be understood through the wall.

Then Doug shouted, "What will she be? A 'zoo-hu' or a 'hu-zoo'?"

Zellie let out a quick laugh before yelling, "OK! OK!" A few moments later, she broke out into song: "Lookin' out, on the morning rain, I used to feel, uninspired."

As he lay in bed, Retina Boy marveled at the depth and force of Zellie's voice. Her singing was hypnotic, as if she could reach into the soul, lock on to it, and not let go. He'd have to ask Ziglo if it was OK to meet her, the Zooban woman who could sing.

Doug and Zellie hadn't been the only reason for Retina Boy's lack of sleep. Ziglo had just told him that the mission to pick up his friends from Earth was moving forward. Retina Boy was anxious for any news on how it was proceeding. Would Marcy actually follow through and bring everyone to the coordinates as he had instructed? Or would she back out because of fear or disbelief? He thought if anyone had the courage to do it, it was she. But there were so many unknowns for her. Retina Boy was certain that Marcy had been racking her brain trying to figure out what was going on—namely what the end game was with the disks and the vigil. For her to follow through with the instructions required a huge leap of faith. But she could be so stubborn and skeptical.

Retina Boy went numb when Ziglo arrived at his cell with Zebnee. No one else from the Zog had ever visited him before. Surely this meant something bad had happened. Maybe Marcy didn't show up at the meeting place. Maybe the spacecraft that had gone to Earth to retrieve them had crashed. Or maybe the Zog had changed their minds, hadn't picked up his friends, and had decided to go with the invasion.

Ziglo said, "Just wanted you to know they're here, and they're doing fine," as he reached out with a bag. "Oh, and I brought you some zoofeejee.

Zolobob's latest recipe. Supposed to be moister, chewier. I haven't tried them yet."

"Really?" Retina Boy asked in shock. "My friends are here?"

"Yes, Zin. Your friends from Earth have arrived," said Zebnee.

The blood from Retina Boy's brain drained to his feet. He became light-headed and wobbly as if he might collapse, so he sat down on the edge of his bed. His mind momentarily went blank.

"Are you OK, Zin?" asked Zebnee after he gave no reply to the news. "Zin? Zin?"

"Yeah, uh... I'm OK," Retina Boy answered hesitantly as he regained awareness. "So where exactly are they?"

"They're here at the Zohag in a different wing," said Ziglo. "They're fine, just sleeping, which they'll do a lot of for a while... you know how that is."

"Uh, yeah," Retina Boy agreed.

"Looks like all five came. Three males, two females. That's what the mission commander told me," Ziglo said as he placed the bag on the table at the foot of the bed. "Don't forget about the zoofeejee. You should eat them while they're still warm."

"Two females?"

"Yes, that's what he said."

Retina Boy couldn't figure out who the second female was. Perhaps they confused Sammy for a woman, because his hair had gotten long, almost down to his shoulders. But then he remembered the "plus one" reference in Marcy's email. Who could the additional person be? As long as Marcy made it, he'd be OK with whoever else came.

"Was one of the females in a wheelchair?" Retina Boy asked.

"A wheelchair? You mean like a scooter?" replied Ziglo.

"Yeah. My girlfriend, Marcy, is paralyzed from the waist down."

Zebnee interjected. "Oh, I think they said one of the females apparently had weak legs and might be using some type of braces to walk. Perhaps that's something we can help her with."

"Oh, she must have had her crutches," said Retina Boy, relieved, remembering that the meeting coordinates were in the middle of a farmer's field so she couldn't have used her wheelchair to get there. Retina Boy smiled, knowing now that Marcy was in fact on Zooba. "I'd like to see Marcy, the girl with the crutches, as soon as I can. She's my girlfriend."

"I'll see what we can do," answered Ziglo. "Shouldn't be a problem."

"We can arrange that," Zebnee concurred.

Zebnee hadn't come with Ziglo to the cell to be social or for anyone's moral support. He was there to inform Retina Boy that the Zog was nervous about how well the Earthlings would acclimate to Zooba and accept the idea of staying long-term to create new hybrid beings—beings who would hopefully have eyesight. There was also the challenge of bringing Zoobans to Earth. No one could predict how Earthlings would respond to alien visitors.

"Look, Zin," Zebnee said. "You need to be aware that the Zog remains anxious about the plan. Our biggest concern is your Earthling friends won't like conditions on Zooba, and they won't cooperate. So we really hope you'll encourage them to give it a little time and let them understand how important they are to us. The Zog expects a lot from you."

The idea that one or perhaps two civilizations rested on his shoulders was surreal to Retina Boy. He didn't disbelieve the circumstances, but they still seemed unreal. At the moment, though, all he could think about was reuniting with Marcy and his friends. He was unable to be concerned with anything else until he was with them again. Once they were all together, he could move forward.

"What about the musical instruments?" he asked, remembering that he had repeatedly requested them. "Did they get some instruments?"

Zebnee was annoyed that Retina Boy changed the subject. "*What instruments?*"

"I specifically asked that your astronauts, or whatever you call them, bring back guitars, keyboards, amps, cables, mikes—all sorts of instruments and gear."

"Oh, he means the musical equipment," Ziglo said reassuringly. "Yeah, they nearly emptied out the vendor you told us about."

"You're kidding! Geez! I didn't need the whole store. I hope the Hawkeye Music Machine has good insurance!"

Chapter 35

Marcy mumbled as she turned her head slowly toward Retina Boy. "Where... uhhhhhhh..." Those were her first words, her first meaningful sign of consciousness since arriving on Zooba.

"It's OK, Marcy. It's OK. It's me. I'm here," Retina Boy said, touching her face as he sat next to her on her narrow Zooban bed. He'd been by her side for an hour or two each day for the last few days. During those visits, he spoke to her, held her hand, and stroked her hair as she lay unresponsive, still recovering from the journey and the long-acting sedation administered by the Zooban space crew. He was relieved to see her finally waking up a little and anxious to tell her where she was, as unreal as it would seem, and the reason for the journey. He'd be careful about telling her too much about her circumstances until she was coherent and oriented. There was so much for her to process and absorb.

He bent over and kissed her on the cheek as he had many times during her first days on Zooba. But with that kiss she smiled slightly, though her eyes remained closed. Retina Boy sensed her happiness and smiled himself. Finally, he knew that she knew he was with her.

A few seconds later, Marcy began muttering again. "Mud... what the... "Then she inhaled deeply, sighed, rolled onto her left side toward her vigilant boyfriend, and fell back asleep.

For Retina Boy, the arrival of Marcy and the band was comforting on multiple levels. Not only was he elated to be in the company of his friends, but he would now also share the still-surreal Zooba experience with other Earthlings. Hopefully they would provide final affirmation that he wasn't crazy and that Zooba was, in fact, an alien planet, with blind inhabitants, on the brink of collapse. And what would his friends see with their eyes? He would undoubtedly learn much more about Zooba from them.

At the same time, Retina Boy was gaining more trust and confidence with Ziglo, Zebnee, and all the other Zooban powers that be given they were able to successfully retrieve his friends. Doing so was certainly no small feat even for an advanced civilization.

Feeling tired and overwhelmed himself, Retina Boy stretched out alongside Marcy on the bed to rest with her until the guards came to take him back to his quarters. Putting his hand on her tummy and his face into her long curls, he was surprised her hair smelled so pleasant after the long trip. There was even a hint of patchouli or perhaps lavender. Her Zooban caretakers must have been grooming or bathing her. He couldn't recall ever being cleaned by anyone when he was recovering from his interstellar journey, but then again, he never felt dirty or unkempt. He found it strange that Zoobans, at least the ones he knew, had strong body odor.

Retina Boy's vigils with Marcy since she had arrived on Zooba elicited a deep love and caring for her he'd never experienced before or at least been aware of. Of course, he'd missed her greatly since his abduction, but to be with her while she slept silently made her seem uncharacteristically innocent and peaceful. Retina Boy knew the first time he met Marcy, after she summoned him from her porch as he walked by on that summer day, that she was a force to be reckoned with. Not only did she draw confidence and swagger from near-genius intelligence, but she also put up an impenetrable wall to hide and deny the wheelchair. Damned be the person to even glance at the clunky hunk of steel and rubber. However, as she lay quiet and motionless, he felt protective, like her guardian.

Dozing off himself, he also wondered what danger he'd put her and their friends in. Perhaps asking them to unwittingly journey to Zooba, to save the dying planet, was selfish, wishful thinking. What had he done? Was he really going to save anyone—Earthlings or Zoobans?

Chapter 36

Marcy couldn't remember the vigil or anything that happened that day. She recalled planning it and being conflicted about whether or not to ask her friends to gather at the mysterious mud circle. "The disks really blew my mind," she said to Retina Boy as she sat up on the bed. She was sharing her cell with Jenny, who was still sleeping much of the time, recovering from the interstellar journey more slowly than Marcy. "I mean... to hear your voice on those disks was wonderful, but I couldn't figure out what was going on, or where you were. It was crazy!"

"I know it must have been really weird. I asked them to send some kind of message, because I just wanted you to know I was OK," said Retina Boy, sitting at the foot of her bed. "I just couldn't tell you that, well... uh... I had been abducted by aliens. They wouldn't let me, and you probably wouldn't have believed it anyway."

"I know. I am having a hard time with what's happened. It really is beyond anything I ever imagined. Being on an alien planet? Really?" Marcy leaned forward, looking intently into Retina Boy's eyes. "But these people, whoever they are, they all have your eyes. It is *so* spooky. They all look sort of like fat, hairy cavemen dressed in robes. And they smell! But they all have your beautiful aquamarine eyes. And they're all blind, like you."

Marcy's observations about Zooba completely jibed with everything that Retina Boy had himself observed and learned from Ziglo. The affirmation was on one hand a relief—he wasn't crazy after all. But it also meant that the Earth invasion was also a real possibility. At the same time, as much as he was going along with the concept of the potential Zooban takeover, he couldn't fully process it; it wasn't sinking in. He told Marcy about the concert, but he was not ready to have the discussion about the Zog's long term plans, especially given that she was still sleeping much of the day and acclimating to the alien surroundings. Furthermore, the Zog would have been very upset if he leaked their plans before they gave him permission to do so.

On the other side of the cell, Jenny sat up in bed—her swollen eyes barely open and her hair covering her face. She looked expressionless at Marcy and Retina Boy for a few seconds and went back to sleep, hugging her pillow.

"So I was wondering something," said Marcy yawning as she lay back down. "Why did these... *Zoobans*... send the disks through *Amazon?*"

"They must have an account, I guess."

Marcy didn't respond. She was unamused and tired.

"Actually, I told them your parents would never open a package addressed to you. But I have no idea how they got the disks into the Amazon system. I guess if they have the smarts to kidnap us, they can deliver a package."

"These onesies are really comfortable," said Jake, trying to make light conversation during a gathering of the new arrivals in the boys' cell. The Zog had separated the five Earthlings by gender—the three males in one cell, Marcy and Jenny in another—but let them hang out together during the day to keep their morale up.

"Yeah, but I don't think this prison inmate look would ever be popular back on Earth," replied Justin. "Dull gray with gross stains isn't exactly attractive. For all we know, the blotches are from Zooban puke."

Everyone looked at Justin in disbelief—they'd never heard him use an untidy word like "puke." Maybe Zooba was giving him an edge. But no one else had anything to add to the mundane conversation. They sat cross-legged in a circle on the floor of the boys' cell, except for Marcy who lay on her side on one of the beds. After a few of these gatherings—and long conversations about their new reality on an alien planet—they didn't have much else to say to one another.

A minute later, Danny stood up and began to walk around the perimeter of the sparse cell, dimly lit by a two-foot-high lamp—a thin vertical shaft that glowed pinkish purple. The room had nothing else but three small beds, each against a wall, two chairs, a sink, and a toilet.

"I can't wait until we get out of this place and go outside," Danny said after bumping lightly into a chair. "It is so fucking dark in here—almost like a cave. With my RP, it's really hard to see. I'm OK when there's normal light. But this darkness all the time is bumming me out."

Marcy sighed. "This whole thing is just so bizarre. I mean, I still can't believe we were abducted. When I got those disks, I really didn't know what to make of them. All I could think was they were some kind of joke. But they had his voice. It was him. I knew it!"

"Yeah, I remember driving out to the farm, but everything else from there is a blank," said Jenny, reclining back on her elbows, shaking her head.

"Sorry, this is all my fault." It was an apology Marcy had been delivering on a continual basis to her friends as they got their energy back.

"Look, Marcy," said Justin. "This isn't your fault. It's nobody's fault. Like you said, it is just bizarre. There's no right or wrong way to handle this kind of thing."

Danny laughed. "Yeah, when we get back to Iowa, you can write to Dear Abby and ask her what the proper etiquette is for inviting your friends to an alien abduction."

"Dear Abby," Jake said in a mocking, church lady voice. "My boyfriend is blind and plays lead guitar in a really cool band. Turns out he is an alien and had me and my friends abducted back to his shithole planet. Should I break it off or just withhold sex for a while? Signed, Human Girlfriend."

Everyone laughed. Even Marcy couldn't hold back a blushing smile.

"Dear Human Girlfriend," replied Danny in an effeminate falsetto. "If he can play decent lead, like Jimmy Page or Slash, and he has a big shlong, I'd stay with him. Just use condoms."

Marcy hurled a pillow across the room at Danny. "You're such an ass."

The humorous moment was much needed for the young Earthlings, who were emotionally overwhelmed by the journey and being in an alien world. However, the Dear Abby exchange raised a question for Jenny she couldn't hold back.

"Marcy, I hope what I am about to ask doesn't put you off, but I can't help myself. Is it weird for you to know that your boyfriend, someone you really love, is so different, that he's not really a human?"

Marcy sat up and didn't hesitate with her reply. "You know, I thought about that when I was waking up and figured out what was going on. I realized what meant most to me was that he was OK, that he was alive. Back on Earth, especially before I got the disks, I wasn't sure I'd ever see him again. That really was the hardest thing."

After Marcy and her traveling companions had recovered from their journey, the Zog decided to keep Retina Boy separated from them much of the time. They didn't want him to reveal—purposely or inadvertently—anything about the Zog's plans other than the concert. Retina Boy and Ziglo eventually got permission to tell the Earthlings they'd also been brought to Zooba for a possible "citizen exchange program" to help the planet recover from the ravages of pollution and overconsumption. Hopefully, humans could teach and inspire Zoobans about recycling and conservation, as well as culture and arts, which could provide an alternative to hoarding material goods. The Zooban love of Earth's Western music, sports, and entertainment were evidence of their potential to grow culturally. And though the Zog recognized Earth had its own environmental issues, they were impressed that some of its leaders and inhabitants were focused on the problems and were trying to implement change. Earth's inhabitants weren't in complete denial like Zooba's had been for so long.

However, the new arrivals from Earth were not informed about the Zog's plan to create a new hybrid species to hopefully bestow eyesight to Zoobans. Even Retina Boy agreed that information would be overwhelming at this early juncture. His friends were just getting used to the idea of being on an alien planet and that their pal Retina Boy was actually Zooban. Also, the Zog hadn't worked out details of who would impregnate whom. They wanted to see how Zellie's progeny turned out before they continued with the cross-species conception experiment.

While having been abducted by aliens and brought to their planet seemed fantastical at first, the new arrivals were not completely surprised to learn that their friend Retina Boy was not human. His luminescent turquoise eyes and ability to navigate without a cane or other assistive devices had made him stand out to most everyone he encountered on Earth. And he had the same nonfunctioning but beautifully mysterious eyes that these aliens had. Jake dubbed Zoobans "the bakery hippies" because of their long hair and beards; dull, tattered clothing; and penchant for snacking on zoofeejee. One guard got confused and perturbed with Jake when he jokingly asked for a Caesar salad for his next meal. "Sorry, dude. I was just kidding," Jake explained. "This croissant thing is cool for me."

Marcy understood that Retina Boy and Ziglo had established somewhat of a trusting relationship but was frustrated by Ziglo's evasiveness when she peppered him with questions about space travel and where in the galaxy Zooba was located. The only clue he gave her was, "We're a lot closer to Earth than you think." However, he did explain that Zooba was much like Earth in terms of circumference, gravity, and atmosphere. It also orbited a star, and one rotation of Zooba took about 15 percent longer than a complete rotation of Earth. He said that while some regions of Zooba were warmer than others, the planet was overall relatively temperate and tilted only slightly on its axis so seasonal changes were minimal.

Ziglo also assured Marcy that she and her friends could likely go back to Earth sometime in the not-too-distant future, though, in truth, that was an issue the Zog hadn't even begun to grapple with.

Knowing that his friends' families would be thrown into turmoil with the disappearance of their sons and daughters, Retina Boy insisted that the Zog allow Marcy and him to produce an audio recording much like the two he'd made for Marcy. The disk would be delivered to his parents, but the message would be sufficiently cryptic so they would have no idea that their son, Marcy, and their friends were on another planet—only that they were safe and well. The Zog agreed to the request, concluding that even if forensic experts on Earth determined that the disk was made of highly sophisticated technologies and materials potentially produced by non-Earthlings, there wasn't much they could do. It wasn't as if Earth's scientists could launch a rescue mission to retrieve them. Of course, they had no idea where Zooba was, and they could barely travel to their lone moon.

The Zog didn't publicly disclose the arrival of the Earthlings nor had they provided any updates to their citizens about invasion plans. However, word of Zellie's pregnancy and that the father was the incarcerated human had leaked out. The forthcoming child created even more conjecture, and Zoobans remained excited about the possibility they could someday soon acquire the ability to see with their eyes.

The Zog, Ziglo, and Retina Boy all agreed that the next crucial step in acclimating the Earthlings to Zooba would be a tour of the local district. The visitors needed to see with their eyes how awful the conditions really were if they were to be convinced to cooperate. Because Zoobans were blind and never saw their troubled planet—before or after the environmental ruin—they were apprehensive about how the Earthlings might see it.

Chapter 37

Marcy marveled at the scooter given to her by the Zohag guards for the tour of the district. It was essentially a tricycle but sleek, as if designed for high-speed racing. It had a thin frame and wheels and was made of ultralight materials; she could lift it easily with one arm. The scooter's controls were four buttons. Two on the left handle bar for acceleration and braking, and two on the right for reverse and a high-pitched horn. However, Marcy was disappointed to learn on the first test drive that it went no faster than walking speed. Nonetheless, she enjoyed taking it for a ride, going back and forth in the hallway outside her cell. Jenny looked on in amusement. It was the first time she'd ever seen Marcy in such a happy, playful mood.

Accompanied by a team of three guards, Jake, Justin, Danny, and Retina Boy joined Jenny and Marcy in the foyer at the Zohag's main entrance. Ziglo and Zebnee arrived shortly after to begin the excursion. All the Earthlings, dressed in dark-gray jumpsuits with masks covering their noses and mouths, were both excited and apprehensive to finally get beyond the confines of the Zohag to experience Zooba and to see firsthand the planet and the environmental problems they'd been hearing so much about.

Shortly after their arrival on Zooba, the Earthlings had been given pen-size flashlights—much improved in luminosity and battery life than the one originally given to Doug—for getting around outside of their cells in the Zohag. But it was midday, so they could navigate easily by ambient light.

Their first few steps out into the district left them with no doubt that Zooba was in serious trouble. They gazed out over a landscape blanketed by ominous thick smog. Only occasional glimpses of a muted lavender sky showed through breaks in the pollution. The commercial sector—bisected by a wide stream of loudly buzzing Zooban pedestrians clad in robes and jumpsuits—was surrounded by hills of discarded consumer products, including furniture, appliances, clothes, and toys. To the Earthlings, it looked as if entire communities had been evicted from their homes, and all their worldly possessions had been dumped onto the massive heaps.

In the distance, sprawling black manufacturing structures billowed out smoke from tall stacks. The factories far outnumbered and overwhelmed occasional air-filtering domes towering into the smog. The bustling commercial sector was split into two large complexes of what looked like public storage units—rows and rows of square and rectangular low-rise storefronts—but completely open, without doors or windows. Most remarkable to the Earthlings was the absence of bright color, lighting, and signage or any other visual information.

The Earthlings were startled by the Zee racing overhead in front of them. The long metallic-looking tube—lacking any windows or portals to see in or out of—looked to them more like a mobile prison or morgue than public transportation.

Marcy had imagined that a highly advanced alien world would be bright and pristine with hundreds of skyscrapers, and that the inhabitants would be zooming around in flying cars and jet packs. She thought the aliens themselves might be diminutive creatures, perhaps with heads, arms, and legs but somehow proportionately different. They might even communicate telepathically and require little sustenance to survive. Zooba was not the alien civilization she had envisioned.

After Zebnee led the group about fifty yards from the Zohag, the "visitors" from Earth stopped and looked at each other in disbelief, hesitant to continue, afraid they'd be forever engulfed in this dystopian world. It was purely an instinctive reaction to perceived danger.

"Holy shit," said Jake from the back of the group. No one else uttered a word.

"Please, let's proceed," said Zebnee, turning around, trying to be reassuring. He knew what the Earthlings saw with their eyes had to be shocking. For a moment he felt deep regret that as a leader of this world he hadn't done more to save it. How had he and the Zog let it come to this?

Despite his own experience of the planet and Ziglo's counseling and their testimonies before the Zog committees, Retina Boy never felt the gravity of the Zooban predicament until now. The arrival of his friends on Zooba was a collision of two worlds, and their reaction to the planet's circumstances made the problems more real to him. He wondered if Zooba could be salvaged. Was it too late for this civilization? Regardless, would Zoobans, without any change in their own habits or culture, bring this same environmental wrath to Earth if they decided to invade?

Just a short time ago, Retina Boy was a carefree blind kid in Iowa with a cute, brainy girlfriend and a halfway decent rock-and-roll band. A promising future stretched out before him, seemingly endless and unobscured. But now he straddled two worlds, both of which were at risk of irreversible calamity. Without any action or intention on his part, he had become an ambassador for saving both planets. He was amazed that he didn't feel more pressure in the role. It still seemed so unreal to him.

The Earthlings and their Zooban escorts moved slowly along the edge of the sector's pedestrian traffic. While what the Earthlings saw of this smoky, dingy metropolis was surreal, they were also fascinated by the myriad strange noises—the thrumming conversations; loud honking, tooting, and beeping; and their own planet's popular music emanating from different directions.

"How the hell did they get that song?" Marcy asked loudly as Stevie Wonder's "Superstition" played from an overhead sound system. Retina Boy had told his friends about Zooba's obsession with popular music and how they intercepted it from Earth's radio broadcasts. His pals were blown away to actually hear it in this bustling alien community. The familiarity of the songs was comforting; it grounded them as they tried to make sense of the strange society they were suddenly immersed in.

"I hear 'Rocket Man!' That's pretty funny," said Danny as the group walked by a zoofeejee vendor unloading a large rack of fresh aromatic pastries from a wide rectangular oven. Jake grinned at Justin. They had both become fans of the Zooban dietary staple while they were in the Zohag. "I say we stop at one of these bakeries for a little midday snack. Wouldn't it be great to get one right out of the oven?" Jake said quietly as he leaned over toward Justin.

Justin nodded in agreement, though he knew that he and his pal would never have the courage to ask for one, especially with no Zooban currency to buy it.

The two became separated from the group after stopping to check out the production of zoofeejee in hopes the vendor might notice them and offer a complimentary sample. They stood at the storefront, intently watching the Zooban baker carefully pull a large sheet of pastries from the oven as the broadcast of "Rocket Man" slowly faded out from the bakery's sound system.

After a few seconds of dead air, "Hey Jude" broke the silence. Paul McCartney's bright iconic vocals immediately enraptured the boys. As they would have back on Earth while in a car, at Java Joe's, or at their own concert, Justin and Jake began to sing along, "Take a sad song, and make it better," as they continued to watch the Zooban baker plucking hot zoofeejee off a tray with gloved hands.

Because their backs were turned to the walkway, the duo didn't realize that pedestrian traffic behind them had come to a complete stop. About two-dozen Zoobans stood in awe, listening to them sing. What they also didn't know was that their live two-part harmony had never before been heard on this planet of twelve billion. In fact, there had never been a public performance of any live music.

A few measures into the song, after "the minute, you let her under your skin, then you begin, to make it better," Justin and Jake stopped singing as the vocal track broke for a short drum riff. They looked at each other, acknowledging they needed to catch up with the rest of the group. The boys turned around and saw their Zooban fans standing motionless, staring with their glowing turquoise eyes as if overcome by some magic spell.

"Whoa, I hope the zombies aren't poised to attack," muttered Jake. Not knowing what strange reaction might come from the onlookers, he and Justin hurried off through the crowd to reunite with the group.

The other Earthlings and their Zooban entourage had been observing the impromptu performance from a distance. Ziglo sensed Zebnee's panic when they first heard the singing, but Ziglo implored him not to react. "It's too late," he said. "Their arrival on Zooba is no longer a secret. It was going to come out sooner or later. Let's try to make the most of the enthusiasm for our visitors."

Chapter 38

News of the Earthlings' brief impromptu "Hey Jude" performance quickly spread across the planet, sparking enormous excitement and a longing for more. Thanks to Ziglo's urging, the Zog agreed to schedule a live Rhodopsin concert as soon as feasible. The performance would be the perfect distraction from the prospects for eyesight and the controversy of a potential Earth invasion that also had Zooba abuzz. As a strategy to begin the promotion of reduced consumption, Retina Boy convinced Ziglo and Zebnee to request a halt in all manufacturing on the days before, of, and after the concert. The Zog liked the idea. If the event was successful, additional concerts and manufacturing moratoriums would be planned around the planet.

Most other elements of the Zog's plan hadn't been worked out yet. But public support for an all-out invasion was waning. Thanks to the "Hey Jude" moment, Zoobans quickly developed affection for the Earth visitors. They were becoming more reluctant to bring harm to their new friends' planet.

A large meeting room on the top floor of the Zohag became Rhodopsin's studio and workshop. The boys dubbed it the "Hawkeye Interstellar Music Machine" or the "Hawkeye" for short as a tribute to the beloved music store back home that had been stripped nearly clean by the Zooban space travelers on the band's behalf. Engineers were enlisted to equip the instruments with power. They attached small long-life power supplies—tiny round gadgets that looked like watch batteries—directly to the power jacks of the gear. The boys were bemused by the Zooban electronics experts who excitedly debated each other about which to use. They'd never worked with guitars or keyboards—or any musical instrument—so were uncertain how much power they consumed.

The engineers were bewildered on one occasion when Jake jokingly suggested, "We can always run out to Radio Shack if we need more batteries." Ziglo, who was standing nearby and becoming attuned to the boys' dry sense of humor, rebutted, "I wouldn't do that if I were you. The guards will demobilize you before you make it three steps out of the Zohag." Jake didn't have the courage to ask exactly how they might demobilize someone attempting an escape. He turned to Justin and whispered, "Yeah, I bet these guys have some badass tasers."

A cadre of ten guards monitored and protected the Earthlings when they gathered in the "Hawkeye" meeting space, though as the band began to practice, another dozen guards usually showed up, merely as spectators. Even though the Zog would launch a publicity campaign once the Rhodopsin concert venue and date were finalized, the band was already the hottest ticket on the planet, with the Zohag guards as their first groupies.

Even though Zellie was more than halfway through her pregnancy, the Zog agreed to Ziglo's request to have her perform a few songs with the band. Having been so impressed with her vocals and wanting a replacement for Sammy, Retina Boy proposed the idea to Ziglo as a way of bringing "one of Zooba's own" into the spotlight. Ziglo agreed with the suggestion, though gently reminding him that he, too, was one of Zooba's own.

Justin needed only an hour to teach Zellie her first song, "Let It Be," a tune she'd already heard a few times and didn't demand much technically. Its melody was simple, and it didn't require a wide vocal range. While the Beatles' beautiful anthemic ballad touched millions back on Earth, Zellie brought a unique spiritual depth and boldness to the song. Even while she was just practicing with Justin, the room went quiet. Zoobans and Earthlings alike were awestruck.

Retina Boy was amazed at how focused the band was on practicing for the upcoming concert. They had few distractions—there was nothing else for them to do but practice. They couldn't go to school, nor were they able to run out for pizza or a movie. They were also feeding off the energy from the Zohag guards, who appeared hypnotized, their mouths agape, as the boys played. Friends and classmates back in Des Moines enjoyed listening to Rhodopsin's respectable covers of popular classic-rock songs, but no one had ever gone gaga over them like the Zohag personnel had.

Retina Boy took pride in how far the band had come since its early days when they blundered through "Smoke on the Water." They were so lost and disjointed back then. Rhodopsin now projected confidence and played as a tight, cohesive unit.

Shortly after the Zooba concert was scheduled, Retina Boy had an overwhelming revelation: Rhodopsin would be playing the first-ever live concert on another planet. The thought of it made his head spin. He felt enormous pressure to get it right—on behalf of humanity and all the rock stars and super groups that came before his modest little cover band. The anxiety was so intense that he never brought it up with anyone else—not even Marcy. He was thankful no one ever mentioned it to him. He knew he'd be OK once they got through the first song. While he did his best to keep the forthcoming gig out of his mind, the anticipation of it continually coursed through his veins.

Chapter 39

Zebnee stood racked with nerves before a crowd of nearly 50,000 excited Zoobans. He was waiting for the go-ahead to introduce the band. With virtually no political forums or cultural events—no rallies, concerts, plays, or other live productions—Zooba didn't have many experienced public speakers or emcees. Retina Boy told the Zog that an introduction from a figurehead was customary, and it would boost excitement for the show. Given that the Zog considered the Rhodopsin concerts to be Zebnee's brainchild, they selected him to introduce the band. "You'll be fine," said Retina Boy, trying to boost the confidence of the Zooban who paced back and forth on the stage as they were setting up for the concert. "Just keep it short and sweet."

The attendees were lucky winners of a ticket lottery for Rhodopsin's concert at the Zola, a dark cavernous amphitheater used long ago by the Zog, when they communicated more openly with the public about key economic, political, and social issues. But the Zog had concluded that transparency mostly roused discord and unrest, stifling their ability to exercise their proconsumption agenda. So rather than debate and negotiate with the masses, the Zog increased production and lowered costs of consumer products. The strategy, in the short run, worked well; Zoobans became obsessed with buying goods and less concerned about having a voice in the political system. In the long run, the policy led to environmental ruin. The Zola was no longer used officially but was still in good repair. Much of the structure was made of a durable synthetic material similar to concrete but softer and more pliable. More recently, it was an unmaintained park for families wanting a respite from the hubbub of the commercial sector. Visiting youngsters loved to scream and shout to hear their echoes and run up and down the amphitheater's long stairways to burn off energy.

In preparation for the concert, engineers installed powerful speakers around the perimeter of the semicircular structure and on the sides of the stage. The sound projected well to all seats but echoed ominously. "Well, it might work well for some of the guitar solos but not so much for the vocals," Retina Boy told one of the lead engineers during the sound check. But he knew nothing more could be done for their first gig at that late juncture. "Maybe we can improve the arrangement of the speakers if we do this again somewhere else."

As Marcy waited with the band at the back of the large open stage for Zebnee's introduction, she gazed up, marveling at the deep-lavender sky that shone through several breaks in the shroud of gray pollution. "It's pretty amazing," she said to Retina Boy. "Just by shutting down their factories for a day or two, the sky is already clearing. I wish you could see it. Zooba has a beautiful atmosphere, almost purple." He didn't reply to Marcy. He just nodded and smiled. He knew what she said was a big deal. Yes, they were already having a positive impact on Zooba's environment. However, at the moment he just wanted to get through his first tune.

The other members of Rhodopsin, clad in gray jumpsuits, looked out in awe of the massive crowd of hairy and robed alien fans, who were buzzing in anticipation of the first-ever public performance of live music on Zooba. Like their audience, Rhodopsin was ready for the show to begin. After spending so much time holed up in the Zohag, the band felt good to be doing what came so naturally—playing live music—even if they were so far away from home in such a strange, unimaginable setting.

What the Earthlings didn't realize was that their performance had already begun to transform the day-to-day life of the planet's inhabitants. In addition to helping clear the air, the moratorium on manufacturing slowed down activity in the commercial sectors. The stoppage gave a majority of Zoobans a vacation—something they rarely got. So they were in an especially pleasant and relaxed mood. Neighbors talked with one another more than usual. Families actually had meals together. And there was great anticipation for the concert. Rarely did Zooban citizens have a special public event to look forward to. It gave them a sense of community and hope.

Finally, the lead engineer walked onto the stage and tapped Zebnee on the shoulder, signaling him to begin his introduction. Zebnee took in a deep breath and stepped forward.

"Welcome fellow Zoobans to this great musical event led by our friends from Earth—Danny, Jake, and Justin, along with Zooban citizens Zin and Zellie," he said, holding a thin microphone, which looked like a baton or wand, just below his mouth, his voice reverberating throughout the dimly lit amphitheater.

The members of the band turned to each other, concerned about the less-than-ideal sound projection.

Zebnee continued, "They call themselves Rhodopsin, which is the name of a chemical in the Earthlings' eyes that enable them to see. They will play ten songs for us. Please remember that on Earth it is customary to put your hands together, like this, after each song to show your gratitude." Zebnee put the microphone in a pocket and clapped his hands a few times to demonstrate. The audience responded with scattered clapping—some practice applause.

As Zebnee moved away from the stage, someone with a deep male voice shouted, "Rock and roll!" from the back of the stadium. A smattering of chuckles came from the crowd.

Zeglo, Ziglo, and Zolobob, who sat near the stage, smiled, feeling confident that the band was going to be a hit—they'd heard them practicing at the Zohag and were impressed.

"What if it's really loud?" Zeglo asked his friends as Rhodopsin took the stage and adjusted and tuned their instruments.

Ziglo replied, "Well, then you'll definitely be able to hear them! Don't worry—they will be great."

At the front of the stage, Retina Boy stood tall with his right foot forward, a brand-new maple-and-black Stratocaster resting on his hip. The energy from the crowd poured over him like a warm, soothing wave. He turned the guitar's volume knob, pumped a wah-wah pedal with his foot, inhaled deeply, and began to pick and bend the first few notes of the "Star-Spangled Banner." The guitar wailed though the amphitheater: *wah, wah-wah, wah, wah, wah*!

Retina Boy had never heard a sound so spacious and omnipotent. To the newly anointed Zooban audience, it felt like the amphitheater was about to rise into the sky. As Justin sat behind his keyboard waiting to play the next song, he imagined that somewhere in the great hereafter, Francis Scott Key and Jimi Hendrix were bumping fists.

What Retina Boy didn't realize was that Zoobans—especially those who avidly listened to radio broadcasts of American sports such as baseball and football—were familiar with the traditional event-opening tune. However, the live and loud psychedelic rendition blew them away. They yelled and gave Retina Boy spirited applause after he completed the brief introductory solo. His electrifying opening performance not only excited the audience, it gave confidence to the rest of the band. They knew their audience was ready to rock.

Rhodopsin's next tune was a six-minute version of "Smoke on the Water," featuring driving solos from everyone, including Justin, who impressed even his pals by banging out uncharacteristically adventurous bluesy riffs. While no one ever questioned his talent or agility, he was the one the band normally called on to lead melodic ballads. However, having programmed his keyboards to sound like a vintage Hammond B3 organ proved to be very inspirational for him. And his energy was infectious, even for Jake, whose voice was strong and gritty despite having limited experience in the role of lead singer. Retina Boy punched Jake's shoulder in approval after the song was over.

Rhodopsin sailed through "Purple Haze" and "Rockin' in the Free World" with their Zooban audience getting more emboldened with clapping and vocal approval. The band's rhythms were infectious for the crowd, with many waving their arms and bobbing their heads to the rhythm. But unlike Earthlings who shouted and screamed, Zoobans let out more of a yowl. Jake would later remark that they sounded like a bunch of mortally wounded cats, but during the show, everyone in the band knew that the newly anointed audience was locked in.

Just like a crowd on Earth, the Zoobans immediately quieted down when Retina Boy switched to acoustic guitar to accompany Justin's mellow vocals in their cover of Pink Floyd's early pastoral tune "Fat Old Sun." Retina Boy picked the audience right back up with the song's concluding electric solo.

Back when Rhodopsin performed their first few shows, Will commented that while they played well, they didn't look lively on stage. Sammy occasionally strutted around to songs with a strong rhythm, but for the most part, the band members huddled over their instruments in deep concentration. Retina Boy never quite got over Will's remark, thinking his band looked boring to its audiences. But he never had the gumption to tell his friends to be more animated. He just wanted them to focus on playing their best. Halfway through the Zooban gig, it occurred to him that they had a blind audience, and whatever they did—or didn't do—onstage would go unseen. The realization was liberating.

When it came time to bring Zellie out for the concert's homestretch, Retina Boy made a last-minute decision not to introduce her until after her first song, "Natural Woman." He wanted to surprise the audience to make the first-ever performance from one of their own even more special.

The young female with long red hair, shimmering blue-green eyes, and plump tummy—an icon of her planet's future—not only delighted her fellow Zoobans, but she also brought many to tears with her urgency and raw emotional power as she sang:

Lookin' out
on the morning rain
I used to feel so
uninspired
And when I knew I had to face
another day
Lord, it made me feel so tired

Before the day I met you,
life was so unkind
But you're the key to my peace of mind

Cause you make me feel
You make me feel
You make me feel like a natural woman

Little did she, the band, or anyone else in the audience know—except
for Ziglo and Zebnee—that the concert was being broadcast throughout
the planet. While Rhodopsin was immediately a huge hit, Zellie's performance would change Zooba's image of itself forever. She became a rare
commodity: a Zooban musical hero. Zellie kept her new fans enraptured as
she sailed through "Let It Be," having gained so much confidence from the
crowd's' boisterous approval of her first tune.

At the request of Retina Boy, Ziglo was able to convince the Zog to let
Doug not only attend the concert, but also come onstage to play a tambourine for one of the songs. Retina Boy felt guilty that Doug received so little
attention from the Zooban authorities. He had not only suffered greatly in
the hands of Zoobans, but he was also the flesh and blood of Retina Boy's
parents. Doug was, for all intents and purposes, his stepbrother. But it was
Retina Boy who had the good fortune of being raised by loving parents and
having a beautiful, supportive community to grow up in.

With the Zooban sun soon setting and darkness overtaking the unlit
amphitheater, Jake signaled Doug to come onstage with a tambourine to
provide rhythmic enhancement to the first half of "Layla." While Doug

followed the rhythm of the tune, he paced back and forth across the right side of the stage, thrusting his head forward as he banged the instrument against his knee. Only Zellie knew that Doug had a penchant for pacing around like a caged animal when he got anxious. To the Earthlings, it was as if he was strung out on PCP or meth and would snap at any moment. His wildness panicked the band.

To make the moment more tenuous, Justin's keyboards were still in Hammond B3 mode when he began the second half of "Layla," which normally featured a long, sweeping classical piano solo. Instead of stopping to troubleshoot the problem—a decision that would have likely made the glitch noticeable and embarrassing—Justin went with the organ sound. To Earth's music fans, the bluesy version of "Layla" would have come across as strange or, at best, ironic. However, most in the Zooban audience didn't notice that something about the tune wasn't right.

Though a little rushed, Rhodopsin finished strongly with Pink Floyd's "Comfortably Numb." Zellie fearlessly delivered the song's iconic high-range vocals:

> There is no pain you are receding
> A distant ship, smoke on the horizon
> You are only coming through in waves
> Your lips move but I can't hear what you're saying
> When I was a child I had a fever
> My hands felt just like two balloons
> Now I've got that feeling once again
> I can't explain you would not understand
> This is not how I am
> I have become comfortably numb

Retina Boy's Stratocaster roared and whined across the amphitheater and beyond as he cranked out the song's ending solo. With sweat dripping from his brow, he pulled and squeezed his guitar strings to extend the echoing wail as long as he could.

Unbeknownst to the band, a few thousand Zoobans had gathered outside the perimeter of the stadium before the concert. Thanks to the engineers who turned up the volume for the finale, "Comfortably Numb" came in loud and clear for them. Many jumped up and down and raised their hands over their heads in delight during Retina Boy's blazing jam.

Though Rhodopsin was just a humble group of impassioned teenage musicians from a small community in Iowa, they had launched the transformation of a planet on the brink of calamity. In a few days, the Zog and Ziglo would receive a report that air pollution had dropped by more than 35 percent during the manufacturing moratorium. While the concert, heard by billions across the planet, wasn't the answer to all of Zooba's environmental woes, it provided a starting point for overcoming them. It provided hope that Zooba could be redeemed.

Chapter 40

Retina Boy paced around the first floor of the medical facility where Marcy was having her spine examined. Zooban doctors were confident they could repair the injury that left her unable to walk. They said that normal mobility usually could be restored, even when the spine was crushed or the cord severed.

The cacophony of hacking and wheezing in the ward was an unsettling reminder of the planet's pervasive respiratory issues. Though no one on Zooba had ever smoked a cigarette, Retina Boy felt as if he was at a chain-smoking convention. He found it ironic that a planet with such serious pollution-related health problems might have the technology to get Marcy out of her chair.

For the last two days, Retina Boy and Ziglo had been hashing out plans for the Earth-Zooba collaboration with a newly formed committee of the Zog. They'd made several major decisions, including the scheduling of a ten-concert tour around the planet with coinciding multiday manufacturing moratoriums. Also, the Zooban electronics gurus were already reverse-engineering musical instruments to produce them on a large scale so that the musicians from Earth, between gigs, could begin teaching young Zoobans how to play. But the negotiations had led to a number of other decisions, as well as a request from the Zog that would be life-changing for both Marcy and Retina Boy. While the Zog's plan didn't come as a surprise to him, he was concerned that Marcy wouldn't agree to it. And what would happen if she said no? Retina Boy decided to wait until she got the spinal exam results before he'd talk to her about the Zog's request. Depending on her mood, maybe he'd wait a few days. He'd returned from the final Zog meeting just before accompanying her to the medical facility and wanted more time to think about how to break the news.

When Marcy came back to the waiting area on her scooter, she put her hand on Retina Boy's knee. But she didn't speak for a few seconds, leading him to think the news from the doctors was not good.

"I can't believe it. They're certain they can help me walk again," she said quietly and slowly. She seemed to be in shock. "The doctors have some type of material to reconnect the severed portion of the spinal cord and reestablish a pathway for nerve signaling. That's what they said."

"Wow, that's incredible!"

"Yeah, and they can definitely repair the bone and cartilage. That's the easy part." Marcy smiled broadly. Somehow, by telling Retina Boy, the good news began to sink in for her. It became real. She was perking up. "I'll need a lot of rehab, months of it, to strengthen my leg and back muscles," she added. "But the exam was so cool. Of course, it was so dark and I couldn't see a thing, but I stood in some sort of compartment, a machine that responded to voice commands in Zooban. And the doctors laughed when it answered back. That kind of freaked me out. But at least they were laughing. When I asked how the machine worked, they told me it was a combination of electromagnetic waves and ultrasound. Pretty cool, huh?"

Marcy leaned over and hugged Retina Boy tightly as if she'd never let go. Noticing a bag on the seat when she finally released him, Marcy asked, "Are those zoofeejee?"

"Yeah, from Ziglo and Zolobob."

"Oh, can I have one? Please. I'm starving. I was in there for a long time."

"Sure," said Retina Boy handing her the bag.

Marcy pulled out a pastry and attacked it as if it were the last one on the planet. "So how did the thing with the Zog go?" she asked as she ate.

"I think it went pretty well. We're going to do about ten concerts. But Zellie may not come because of the baby, at least until it's born."

"Well, that makes sense," said Marcy, taking another bite.

"Yeah, it definitely does."

Marcy waited for Retina Boy to continue recapping the meeting.

"So what else?" she asked, having become impatient. "There must have been more that happened."

"Yeah, quite a bit. And some of it involves you."

"Really?" Marcy stopped chewing.

"Yeah, uh, first of all, they want you and Jenny to be liaisons for the communications back to Earth. Eventually, they want you to help set up the exchange of Zoobans and Earthlings. But that won't happen for a while."

"Really? Wow!" The role wasn't exactly the space research she hoped to do, but it was perhaps more important. She would be excited to tell everyone back home about Zooba, including its advanced technologies as well as its environmental predicament. "Maybe Jenny and I can set up an audio blog or a website at Berkeley with daily reports or something."

"Sure. That's a great idea," said Retina Boy.

"So did they say anything about when we can go back to Earth?" Marcy asked, knowing that he and Ziglo planned to discuss the issue with the Zog. Shortly after the concert, she and the others had made it clear they were anxious to get back home, at least to visit for a while.

"They said they can definitely get you home at some point, but they aren't sure when. However, they *did* say they'd take you into space and show you some moons and planets in their solar system. The only problem is they need to find or build a portal for you to look through. They think there may be some translucent paneling near a solar energy module on some of their spacecraft."

"That would be awesome!" Marcy said, her face lighting up. "What about a space walk? Can they let me do that, too?"

"Honestly, I don't know. We didn't get that far in the discussion," said Retina Boy, a little annoyed. "But I think it's pretty cool they're going to build you a window in one of their ships... if they need to."

"Yeah, you're right," Marcy replied, realizing that she was perhaps expecting too much. After all, just a few minutes ago she learned that the Zoobans would enable her to walk again. That in itself was more than she could have ever asked for.

Retina Boy decided he couldn't wait to tell Marcy what the Zog wanted most. No time was going to be perfect. And she was in a rather good mood. Great news had just come her way.

"So, Marcy, there's one more thing the Zog is asking us for, and I'm just going to put it out there." Retina Boy sighed. "They want me to impregnate you."

"Impregnate?"

"Yeah, they want us to have a baby to see if it will have eyesight. Maybe a couple of kids. Maybe more."

"Impregnate?"

"Yeah." Retina Boy was flummoxed, waiting for Marcy to explode.

"I hate that word. It sounds like we'd be a science experiment."

"Sorry, that's just what the Zog calls it," said Retina Boy. "I know it isn't romantic. I'm really, really sorry... really."

The news wasn't a surprise to Marcy. With all the hoopla surrounding Zellie's pregnancy, she expected for some time that she and Retina Boy would be asked by the Zog to conceive a child. It made sense for them to be part of the scientists' vision experiment.

Marcy leaned forward and kissed Retina Boy softly on the lips. Then she placed her hands on his shoulders and watched his eyes as they darkened to indigo. "Sure, let's do it," she said. "I never thought I'd be so happy to be kidnapped by blind aliens, brought to their environmentally ravaged planet, and then *impregnated* by their only rock star."

Chapter 41

Kathy Downs stood outside Eduardo Molina's room as two young men from the Ramon Funeral Home—tall, head-shaven brutes dressed in navy pants and dark-gray polo shirts—slowly guided a gurney in through the doorway to retrieve him. Nearly twenty of Mr. Molina's family members and friends had packed the small room to say goodbye to him and provide comfort to Christina, his wife of thirty-five years. She wept as most of the visitors left the room to make way for the retrieval of the body. Eduardo had been a maintenance man at a local elementary school. His wife said that he had never been by himself for the four days he was in the hospice inpatient unit. She had wanted to keep him at home, but his unbearable pain required round-the-clock management.

"Oy," Kathy blurted to herself as she glanced down at Eduardo's chart, realizing she'd forgotten to write down his time of death. She scrolled through the sent calls on her smartphone and saw that she called Ramon at one thirty, so she estimated that Mr. Molina had passed at around one twenty. She wrote "1:21 p.m." in the file.

Often when Ramon came to the unit, Kathy recalled her second day of hospice-care training the prior year, when Lori, the unit social worker, had mentioned it was funny that all the Latino families liked to use Ramon for their deceased loved ones, yet the funeral home owners were of Norwegian descent. "Yeah, Ned Ramon confessed to me that he doesn't tell anyone they have Norwegian heritage because he doesn't want to lose the Spanish business," Lori had said when showing Kathy the listing of local funeral homes. "But everyone in town knows the Ramons are Weegies, so there yuh go!"

After more than two decades as an RN in the hospital—first with neo-nates and then on the med-surg unit—hospice care was a pleasant, slower change of pace for Kathy. Care was less complicated for the terminally ill. Most patients on the unit needed only pain management. Some had difficulty breathing. Morphine usually helped with both symptoms. Patients whose cases became more complicated were sent to the main hospital across the street.

With their twin daughters heading off to college soon in Lincoln, Kathy and her husband, Don, were planning more vacations, including an RV trip out west to visit the Grand Canyon, Zion, and several other national parks, and the hospice unit gave her more flexibility with her schedule. In another year or two, she might even go part-time.

As she walked over to the nurses' station to type up the death certif-icate, a man and woman in dark suits emerged from the sliding doors of the unit's main entrance. They stopped briefly, scanned the surroundings, and then walked toward Kathy. Both were middle-aged, nondescript, with stoic expressions, as if they had serious business to attend to. To Kathy, they looked more like lawyers or financial advisors than the usual family members of patients. However, visits from business or legal professionals were rare.

"Hello, we are looking for Ms. Kathy Downs," the man said. "We understand she is in the facility today."

"Well, I'm Kathy. Is there something I can help you with?"

"Yes, Ms. Downs," the man responded quietly, handing her his business card. "I'm Paul Bennett and this is Jean Bernstein. We are special agents from the Federal Bureau of Investigation, and we'd just like to talk with you for a few minutes, if we can. Is now a good time? Sorry to bother you."

"Uh, yeah, sure. Let's go into this meeting room over in the corner," Kathy replied, pointing to her left.

"Holy shit," she muttered to herself as she followed several steps behind them. Kathy couldn't imagine what the FBI would be investigating. Had one of the staff been caught stealing morphine? And why would they want to talk to her? Except for smoking a little pot every year or so at a party, she and Don had been upstanding citizens; they cut their lawn and paid their taxes.

After she and the agents entered the room, Kathy said, "Please wait here a moment while I let Wanda, our nursing assistant, know I'm busy. I'll be back in a sec."

But Kathy saw Wanda had been watching the events unfold from the doorway of a patient's room, so she just pointed to the two guests sitting at the table to indicate she would be with them. Wanda, looking puzzled, nodded. Kathy went back into the meeting room, shut the door, and sat down across from the agents.

Agent Bernstein put her hands on the table. "First, you should know that you are not under investigation for any criminal activity," she said. "We just have a few questions for you."

"OK, but can I ask what the investigation, or whatever you are doing, is all about?"

"Sorry," said Agent Bernstein shaking her head. "At least at this point we can't disclose anything."

"OK," Kathy replied, sitting back in her chair—relieved and perplexed. "I guess I'll do the best I can to help."

Agent Bernstein nodded and smiled. "Thank you."

Agent Bennett flipped a page over on his small notepad, took a pen out of his shirt pocket, and looked up intently at Kathy. "Do you recall where you were employed during the summer of 1996?" he asked.

"Uh, sure. I worked in the nursery at the hospital across the street. Back then it was Polk County. I worked the overnight shift."

Agent Bennett nodded but didn't write anything down. "Do you recall working the night of June 3rd and the early morning of June 4th?"

"Not exactly, but if those were weekdays, I was probably there. I worked weekday night shifts."

Agent Bennett nodded again without writing anything on his notepad. "You don't happen to recall a patient, a boy born on June 3rd, by the name of Doug Anderson?"

"No, not off the top of my head," Kathy answered as she looked at Bennett and then at Bernstein. "But wait," she added as she stretched her arms out on the table, pressing her palms and fingers down. "Wasn't that the name of the blind kid who went missing last March?"

The FBI agents looked at each other, unsure of what their next question would be or who would ask it.

Author's notes

This book is dedicated to all individuals and families with challenging visual impairments. I am especially grateful to those with retinal degenerative diseases such as retinitis pigmentosa, Leber congenital amaurosis, Usher syndrome, Stargardt disease, and age-related macular degeneration. As a writer for the Foundation Fighting Blindness, I've had the privilege of interviewing dozens of people and families impacted by these retinal conditions. While I fully embrace the Foundation's mission to eradicate all retinal degenerative diseases, "*Retina Boy*" is an homage to those who persevere and thrive despite having few treatments or cures for their vision loss. Their courage, resourcefulness, and resilience have been incredibly inspiring for me. They are my heroes.

I've also had the privilege of reporting on retinal research advancements for emerging therapies to save and restore vision. It has been a fascinating journey. I'd like to thank the following investigators for enlightening me, a nonscientist, about the retina and related research:

Gus Aguirre, Rando Allikmets, John Ash, Isabelle Audo, Radha Ayyagari, William Beltran, Jean Bennett, Paul Bernstein, Eliot Berson, David Birch, Dean Bok, Shannon Boye, Craig Beeson, Kari Branham, Dan Chung, Artur Cideciyan, Dennis Clegg, Jason Comander, Frans Cremers, Stephen Daiger, Jill Dolgin, John Dowling, Jacque Duncan, Jane Farrar, Gerald Fishman, John Flannery, Peter Francis, David Gamm, Mort Goldberg, Sandeep Grover, Karina Guziewicz, William Hauswirth,

Dennis Hoffman, Mark Humayun, Alex Iannoccone, Sam Jacobson, Christine Kay, Bill Kimberling, Henry Klassen, Alan Laties, Matt LaVail, Jennifer Lentz, Ray Lund, Ian MacDonald, Robert MacLaren, Al Maguire, Michel Michaelides, Muna Naash, Kris Palczewski, Mark Pennesi, Eric Pierce, Barb Rohrer, José Sahel, Tim Schoen, Hendrik Scholl, Johanna Seddon, Dror Sharon, Ed Stone, Tim Stout, Janet Sunness, Karmen Trzupek, Dick Weleber, Michael Young, Don Zack, and Marco Zarbin.

Special thanks to Diane Luchese for superb editing.

Thanks to David Pace and Kathryn Johnson for helpful feedback and editing.

About the Author

Ben Shaberman's books include Jerry's Vegan Women (fiction) and The Vegan Monologues (collected essays), both of which were published by Apprentice House, Loyola University Maryland. His essays, articles, and commentaries have been carried by several prominent media outlets including: The Washington Post, Chicago Tribune, The Baltimore Sun, Des Moines Register, VegNews, Sky and Telescope Magazine, and NPR. Shaberman's fiction and creative non-fiction have been published in a number of journals and blogs including: The Artist Unleashed, Empty Mirror, Months to Years, The Good Men Project, and Clean Sheets Erotica Magazine. He earned a master of arts in writing (poetry) from Johns Hopkins University. Shaberman is the senior communications director and science writer at the Foundation Fighting Blindness.

Apprentice
House Press
Loyola University Maryland

Apprentice House is the country's only campus-based, student-staffed book publishing company. Directed by professors and industry professionals, it is a nonprofit activity of the Communication Department at Loyola University Maryland.

Using state-of-the-art technology and an experiential learning model of education, Apprentice House publishes books in untraditional ways. This dual responsibility as publishers and educators creates an unprecedented collaborative environment among faculty and students, while teaching tomorrow's editors, designers, and marketers.

Outside of class, progress on book projects is carried forth by the AH Book Publishing Club, a co-curricular campus organization supported by Loyola University Maryland's Office of Student Activities.

Eclectic and provocative, Apprentice House titles intend to entertain as well as spark dialogue on a variety of topics. Financial contributions to sustain the press's work are welcomed. Contributions are tax deductible to the fullest extent allowed by the IRS.

To learn more about Apprentice House books or to obtain submission guidelines, please visit www.apprenticehouse.com.

Apprentice House
Communication Department
Loyola University Maryland
4501 N. Charles Street
Baltimore, MD 21210
Ph: 410-617-5265 • Fax: 410-617-2198
info@apprenticehouse.com • www.apprenticehouse.com

CPSIA information can be obtained
at www.ICGtesting.com
Printed in the USA
LVHW021358160720
660844LV00009B/467